THE
WHISPER
HOUSE

THE
WHISPER
HOUSE

DAWN MERRIMAN

SECOND SKY

Published by Second Sky in 2024

An imprint of Storyfire Ltd.
Carmelite House
50 Victoria Embankment
London EC4Y oDZ
United Kingdom

www.secondskybooks.com

ISBN: 978-1-83525-071-6
eBook ISBN: 978-1-83525-070-9

This book is dedicated to my husband, Kevin.
Thank you for all your help and your constant support. I could not tell these stories without you.

ONE

RYLAN FLYNN

"What do you think he wants?" Aunt Val asks as she throws George's ball into the yard. We watch the big black dog bound after the toy.

"With Declan, it's hard to tell. But he thinks his mansion is haunted and wants me to check it out." I lean back in my rocking chair on Val's front porch as the sun sets behind the trees. I'm snatching a few moments of peace before I have to pick up Mickey and make the drive to my ex-boyfriend's house. Ever since I got the call two days ago, I've been dreading this evening. I had planned on never seeing Declan Rathborne again. For two years, I've managed that just fine, even living in a town as small as Ashby, Indiana.

"You think his house is really haunted?" Val asks. "That could be interesting." George drops the ball at her feet.

"All my cases are interesting. It will be nice to make a new episode though." Our YouTube show *Beyond the Dead* has been pulling in new viewers recently, but that just means the pressure is on for new content. Filming at Declan's old mansion should give us some good shots, whatever we find there.

If only Declan wasn't going to be there.

I put my black sneakers on the porch railing and tip my chair back. Behind the trees, the sun is flaming. Snippets of pink and red flicker through the branches.

So does a dark shadow.

I drop my feet and sit forward. "Did you see that?"

Val is fishing under her chair for George's ball, but looks up at my question. "See what?" she asks, an odd hesitation to her voice.

"I thought I saw something." I scan the trees for the moving shadow, my back tingling. A spirit is near. "I feel like something is out there."

A sick déjà vu washes over me. I don't want to see a ghost here again. Aunt Val's cabin is supposed to be my safe space.

Val finds George's ball, but doesn't throw it for him. She looks at the trees, her eyes squinting a little.

"I don't see him."

I turn to look at her. "Him?"

"I—I mean it could be a him." She gives the ball to George, then pats his head.

"I suppose." I cross the porch and start down the steps.

"You're not going into the woods are you?"

"I just want to check it out." I take a few steps across the grass, looking for the shadow that has slipped behind a tree. It couldn't have gotten too far; I still feel the tingles.

"Rylan, you don't have time for this. You have a show to tape tonight."

I stop and look back to the porch. Aunt Val stands in the last of the setting sun, her blonde hair glowing pink from the light.

I'm torn. She's right, but I'm super curious about what I saw in the trees.

"I'm sure it was just the light playing tricks on your eyes," she says, dismissing my concerns and throwing George's ball my direction. It bounces a few feet away and George hurries off the porch toward it.

Looking to the trees again, I don't see the shadow shape. The tingle in my back is gone too. "I suppose you're right." I pull my phone from my pocket and check the time. "I need to go pick up Mickey, anyway."

Val descends the three steps from the porch to my side. She gives me a quick hug. "Good luck tonight. With the ghosts and with Declan."

"Ghosts I can handle. The other, I'm not so sure about."

"He's just a guy. A scared guy at that, if he's calling you about a haunting."

"I'll be fine. It's just a job." I stare into the woods again. "I really thought I saw something in there," I add.

Val turns toward the trees then crosses her arms over her chest. When she faces me again, her face is pinched. She opens her mouth as if to say something, then changes her mind.

George is at her legs with the ball. She takes the toy and throws it across the yard, the moment past.

"I'm going," I say.

"Stop by the shop tomorrow. I want to hear all about tonight."

"I will," I promise as I climb into the old tan Cadillac I inherited from my mother. When I check the rearview, I expect her to be watching me leave. Instead, she's walking toward the trees. When I round a bend, she disappears from sight.

———

"You scared?" Mickey asks as we drive past freshly planted fields and tree lines just beginning to bud. The moon is huge and hangs low and lovely. Even the pretty sky can't calm my nerves.

"Why do you ask?" I play dumb.

"Because you're driving really slow."

I check the speedometer and she's right, I'm going half the

speed limit. I push the gas a little harder. "I'm not scared of Declan Rathborne."

"I would be. You were a mess when he broke up with you."

"I broke up with him," I remind her. "And I wasn't a mess."

"Okay," she concedes. "Maybe not a mess, but you were upset."

I chew on my bottom lip, debating on how much to say. I never told Mickey the whole truth about the end of Declan and me. I really don't want to get into it now, while we're driving to his house.

"There's the house." I'm thankful I can change the subject. Truth is I am a little scared. Not of the ghosts he thinks might be haunting him, but of seeing the only serious boyfriend I've ever had.

But he called with a ghost problem and I can't turn that down, especially since we'll be filming in the historic Krieger Mansion. The massive, three-story brick home, topped with two lovely turrets, is the largest in all of Northeast Indiana. It's a local landmark and a wonderful place to film for our ghost encounter show. I remember wondering as a child what the view from the turrets must be like. I could picture myself sitting in one reading a book. The clouds gathering in the west make the house seem even more imposing.

"I can't believe we're going to go inside," Mickey says with a touch of awe as we drive down the tree-lined lane leading to the historic home, which looks more like a museum than a private residence. Thick woods crowd close to the back of the house. A garden, more reminiscent of an English estate than Ashby, Indiana, fills the side yard. The entire place feels like another place and time. "Declan must be doing well with his writing to live here," Mickey says.

I grip the steering wheel, wanting to put the car in reverse and drive away. When we were dating, Declan was an aspiring writer of mystery novels. I heard from Aunt Val that he landed a publishing deal and has gone on to write several books.

Judging by his home, Declan did all right. Of course, his mother came from money, which helps.

"It's not that great," I lie. Even in the dark, the house is imposing. The bright moon reflects on the many windows trimmed in white. I feel like the house is staring at me.

"Far cry from the apartment he had when you were dating," Mickey says as I park the Cadillac in the circle drive.

I look out the windshield and up the three levels of brick to the turrets at the top. I can't imagine Declan living here all alone.

"You think he has staff?" Mickey asks. "This is a lot of house to keep up."

"He has to. That's a lot of cleaning. Not to mention the garden." I'd rather talk of dusting than of the man I'm about to see.

I run a hand down my long brown hair, smoothing it into place. I resist the urge to check my reflection in the rearview mirror.

"Ready?" I ask.

The massive front door suddenly swings open and Declan steps out into the evening, the porch light reflecting off his dark hair.

"Phew, I forgot how handsome he is. Almost as cute as Marco," Mickey says, mentioning her husband.

"He's not that great," I say, trying not to look. Declan Rathborne has the classic good looks and air of money that most women find irresistible. Add the lilting South African accent, from growing up in Cape Town with his father, and he's what some would call a catch.

He smiles, straight white teeth flashing.

I don't immediately climb out of the car, but Mickey opens her door. "Declan, good to see you."

"So nice to see you again, Mickey," he lilts.

My stomach churns and my back tingles. I focus on the tiny tingle, hoping for the distraction of a ghost nearby.

I stay in the car as long as I can without being rude, then open my door. It squeals as it slides open and I am mortified by the ancient car. Declan loved cars and I imagine by now he has several.

I bet none of his fancy cars squeal when the door opens.

His welcoming smile seems genuine when I dare to look at his face. The crinkles at the corners of his brown eyes are deeper than I remember, but other than that he looks the same.

I smooth my hair again as I walk around the car toward his outstretched hands. I can't avoid the handshake and let him take mine for a brief moment. His palm is damp. I wonder if he is as nervous about this reunion as I am.

"So glad you came, Rylan," he says warmly, his eyes searching for mine. I don't meet his gaze. He takes the hint and turns to Mickey. "You brought your camera?"

"Sure did." Mickey opens the back door to the Cadillac and takes out the bulky camera. "You really think this house is haunted?" Mickey looks up at the brick again. "I can believe that."

Declan looks to me. "You'll have to tell me. But I hear things sometimes. Groans and moans. A few times I heard screams. Like someone is in pain."

"That could be the house settling. Old place like this probably groans a lot," I say, not sure why I feel like discrediting a ghost encounter. I never do that to clients.

But Declan isn't a regular client.

"I know that," he says tightly. "This is different."

Declan and I dated for only six months or so before I broke it off with him. One of the major issues we had was what I did for a living. He didn't fully believe in ghosts, even when he watched footage from our show. I always got the feeling he thought I was a fraud.

Now he's asking me for help. It's a bit much to take in.

"We'll see," I say, with a little too much snark. I instantly regret my tone. He must be in a bad way if he called me after two years of radio silence.

Mickey gives me a pointed look. "Where do you want to start?" she asks, saving the conversation.

"Let's take a look around first. See if I get anything."

Declan eyes me curiously. "Do you? I mean, do you sense something?"

I take a moment to consider, to listen to my body, to feel for tingles. Besides the butterflies in my stomach from this crazy situation, I don't really feel anything substantial. The tiny tingle is gone.

"Nothing yet," I say. Declan looks disappointed. "Maybe once we're inside," I add.

He steps across the paving stones to the heavy doors. "We have the house to ourselves," he says. "I sent Anita way for the night."

I exchange a look with Mickey. "Anita?"

"The live-in housekeeper." There's just a hint of arrogance to his words.

"A housekeeper?" Mickey asks, impressed.

"Does Anita hear things too? Does she think the house is haunted?" I ask.

Declan looks confused, his hand turning the door knob. "I've never asked."

I resist the urge to roll my eyes as I follow through the open door.

The entry to Krieger Mansion is as impressive as the outside. Dark wood walls gleam in the light of a massive, glittering chandelier. A wide staircase curls up the wall to a second-floor landing.

"Wow, nice," Mickey says.

"It is, isn't it," Declan says with obvious pride. "The wood-work is all hand carved from lumber they sourced from the woods behind the house."

Mickey runs a hand across the stair rail, gazes in wonder at the chandelier.

I stand in the middle of the entry. Now that we are inside, I feel tingles in my lower back. A sure sign there's a ghost nearby.

Declan looks to me for my reaction to his house. "It's very nice," I say non-committally. The tingle in my back is growing to an ache. I rub my lower spine.

Mickey turns, sees me rubbing. "There's one here, isn't there?" She pulls her camera to her shoulder.

The sensation is so strong it's making me a little nauseous. I nod. "Something is here."

Declan looks from me to Mickey. "Really? There's a ghost here?"

"Somewhere close." I pull my hand from my back. "Show me where you hear the sounds the most."

Declan glances at the camera. "You're filming already?"

"I told you we'd come if we could film for the show," I say.

"I—okay. I guess that's fair."

"The sounds?" I prompt.

"Mostly I hear them at night. Often in the kitchen." He leads us down a dark hall from the entry. I follow with Mickey right behind me. Soon we enter a kitchen that doesn't seem to match the house we've seen so far. Gleaming stainless steel and white tile fill the room.

"I re-did the kitchen soon after I bought the place," Declan explains. "Brought it up to date."

The kitchen looks like it should be in some interior design magazine, but it's entirely not my style. I wish we could have seen it in its original state.

Mickey pans the camera all over the room and I stand near the white-marble island in the middle, looking around.

"Is that a dumbwaiter?" I ask, crossing to the wall and running my fingers over the buttons that send the small elevator to other floors.

"Yes, I kept that. It was just too cool." He opens the door to the dumbwaiter and I look inside. The original equipment looks out of place in the almost futuristic kitchen.

I step back and he closes the door.

"So, anything?" he asks.

The ache in my back has eased. Whatever Declan thinks he's heard in this space, there isn't a ghost here now.

"I don't think there's anything in here," I say.

"Really?" Declan asks in surprise. "I've heard moaning in here lots of times."

"Old plumbing maybe? I don't know, but I'm not getting anything from here. I don't see anyone."

"Want to try another room?" Mickey asks from behind the camera.

A rhythmic clicking noise floats down the hall. Mickey and I turn toward the sound.

"Is there someone else here?" I ask.

TWO

RYLAN FLYNN

"It's just us," Declan says. He seems unconcerned. "Must be Evie."

Before I can ask who Evie is, a tiny chihuahua darts into the kitchen and begins barking. The tan and black dog bounces she's barking so hard at Mickey and me.

"Evie, stop that," Declan commands.

Evie isn't interested in listening. She carries on letting Mickey and me know we are not welcome.

"Hey, Evie," I say in a high voice, hoping to make friends. She quiets for a moment, and looks at me. "That's a good girl."

The tiny dog looks to Declan then back to me. She barks once more, then must realize we are not a threat. I crouch in front of her and put my hand out for her to sniff.

Evie takes the offered friendship and sniffs the tips of my fingers.

"Sorry about that," Declan says. "I thought she was locked in my room upstairs."

"She's cute," I say. "I didn't know you had a dog."

"I got her last summer. She's a good watch dog." His words

are tinged with humor. "She doesn't know she's so little. She thinks she's big."

Mickey has turned off the camera and crouches next to me. "Here girl." She, too, reaches out her hand. Evie sniffs her fingers then licks the back of her hand.

"She likes you, Mickey," Declan says in surprise. "She's not the most social animal, but I love her."

Mickey rubs the back of Evie's tiny neck. "I wish we could have a dog, but Marco is allergic," she says with a tinge of wistfulness.

Declan picks Evie up and cradles her against his chest. "Now, Evie, we have work to do. You need to be good." He pets her on the head with obvious affection. For the briefest of moments, I remember why I liked him.

"Do you want to look around the rest of the house to see what we might find?" Mickey says, picking up her camera.

"I'd love to see the turrets," I offer.

"This way." With Declan snuggling the tiny dog, we follow him through the house. I'm happy to see the rest of the décor is still original. Dark wood paneling adorns nearly every wall. Declan turns on lights as we make our way around, but the old fixtures don't do much to dispel the shadows.

"Anything?" Declan asks as we climb the steps to the third floor. The crushing pressure in my back from earlier is gone, I still feel a tiny tingle in my spine.

"Just a little," I say with disappointment. "I can't really say yet." I was sure this house was haunted. It looks like a typical haunted house.

"This was the servants' quarters," he says when we reach the third floor. "Now Anita lives up here in an apartment."

"Do you have any other help besides the groundskeeper? A place like this is a lot to take care of," Mickey asks.

"Keith takes care of the property, the garden, the yard, that sort of thing. He lives in a cottage near the woods. Then Anita and that's it."

I'm not really listening, I'm focusing on the house, on the energy of the place. I'm sure there's a spirit of some sort around, but I can't get a good read on it. We look in each room as we go, but I don't see anything otherworldly. I wonder if the spirit is hiding or if it is just too weak for me to see.

We reach a door at the end of the hall and Declan stops. "These are the steps to the turret at this end of the house. Maybe we'll get lucky here." He doesn't sound like he believes I'll see anything. "We'll see, won't we," he says to Evie tucked in his arm.

Ghost or no ghost, I'm excited to go up into the small room at the top of the house. "May I?" I ask, reaching for the door knob.

"By all means," Declan says, stepping back.

I turn the knob and open the plain door. Musty air greets my nose. "When's the last time you had this door open?"

"I'm not sure I've ever opened it," he says.

"Never?" Mickey says.

Declan looks uncomfortable, and I remember he is afraid of heights. I'm anxious to see the view from way up here. Indiana is flat land and we don't often get a birds-eye view of anything.

"Coming?" I ask Mickey and start up the narrow steps.

"We'll just wait here," Declan says, petting Evie.

Mickey is right behind me as we reach the round, all-glass room. "Wow, what a view," I say, looking across the fields. Lights from farmhouses dot the landscape, tiny islands in the darkness.

Mickey films out the windows capturing the dark fields, then turns the camera on me. "Any spirits?"

I'm suddenly nauseous from a strong tingle. "There's something here."

Mickey focuses on my face. I talk to the camera. "I'm

sensing a strong presence here. I can feel it in my back." I actually feel it everywhere now. I slowly spin around in the cramped space, wondering where the spirit is.

A shape flickers to my right. A Black woman in an old-fashioned dress appears.

"Hello," I say quietly. She looks from me to Mickey, then down the stairs.

"You find anything?" Declan calls up the steps.

The shape flickers away.

So do the sensations in my body.

"There was a woman," I tell the camera and Declan. "She was here for just a moment, but she's gone now."

"Gone as in crossed over?" he asks from the floor below.

"No, just gone."

Declan grumbles.

Mickey turns off the camera and removes it from her shoulder. "She's really gone?"

"She just flickered then disappeared," I say, looking down to the ground. No wonder Declan never comes up here. The view is making my head spin a little.

From here, we can just make out the hedges and borders of the garden. As I watch, a dark shape moves between two shadows. It is only there for a moment. But it seems much more solid than the shape I saw at Val's.

"Did you see that?" I ask Mickey.

She presses her face near the glass. "See what?"

"Something's moving down there." I see the shape again as it moves jerkily through the garden.

"I see it." She squints into the dark. "A deer maybe?"

"I don't think so. It looks like a person." I call down the stairs to Declan. "Is there any reason someone would be in your garden?"

His face appears at the bottom of the steps. "No. Why?"

I look back to the garden. In the moonlight, I can see the

shadow is flat on the ground. "I think someone is out there." I descend the steps so quickly I almost fall down them. Evie growls at my agitation.

"There's definitely something out there," Mickey says when we reach the third-floor hall.

Declan seems confused. "Why would someone be in the garden?"

"Let's go find out," I say and hurry down the hall.

"Is that safe?" he asks, trailing after me, fear making his voice raise.

This gives me pause.

"What if it's a prowler?" Mickey asks.

I stop at the top of the stairs leading to the second floor. Maybe she's right.

A scream from outside makes my feet move. "Someone is in trouble out there." I run down the stairs and through the second-floor hall.

"Take these steps instead," Declan says. "They lead to the kitchen and out to the garden."

Another scream, weaker this time, comes from the yard.

Mickey and I follow Declan down the back stairway, through the kitchen, to a door that leads outside.

I reach to open the door.

"Wait," Mickey says. "This could be dangerous. We don't know who is screaming or why." Her eyes are huge with fear.

"She has a point," Declan says, his eyes as big as Mickey's.

"What if someone is in trouble?" I ask.

"Maybe we should call the police instead," Mickey says, grabbing my shirt sleeve, making my charm bracelet jingle.

"It will take them a while to get way out here," I point out.

"Wait," Declan says running to the kitchen counter. He puts Evie down, then grabs knives from the block on the counter. "Take these. We don't know what's out there."

Mickey darts her eyes to me in question. "Knives?"

There's no time to argue. And Declan is right—anyone or anything could be out there in the dark. I take the largest knife. "Come on, someone's in trouble."

Mickey takes the smallest one. "Okay."

Declan opens the door and we hurry outside.

THREE

RYLAN FLYNN

"Where did you see someone?" Declan asks as we hurry into the backyard.

"In the garden." I peer into the dark. The large moon is now hidden behind gathering clouds.

"I heard something," Mickey says, pointing with her tiny knife. "Over there."

I jog in that direction, pulling my phone from my pocket and turning on the flashlight. I scan the garden paths with it, wishing the moon would come out. But it's starting to rain and the sky is heavy with clouds.

The rising wind carries a low moan to us.

I shine the light in that direction and it bounces off red poppies. The bright color startles me for a moment, then I see her.

A woman lies on the path, her body covered in blood more red than the poppies.

"Holy flip," I shout, dropping my knife and sprinting to her side. Once I reach her, I'm not sure what to do. My hands shake as I give my phone to Declan. "Here, hold the light."

I suddenly want Ford. He'd know what to do. I hear his voice in my head, *"pressure."*

The woman's shirt is soaked. There is so much blood I don't know where to press first.

"I'm calling 911," Mickey says in a panic, the wind carrying her voice away.

Declan stands in shock, holding the light on the woman, but saying nothing. I look to him for help, but he's frozen still, his eyes huge with fear.

The woman opens her eyes and they lock on me. "Help..." she groans, then her eyes roll back in her head.

"Stay with me," I tell her, kneeling by her side, searching for the source of the bleeding. I find a slash in her chest that is spurting. Amazingly, she has a bandage on the wound already, but it has come loose. I grab the soaked pad and shove hard against the wound. Hot blood seeps between my fingers, spurting with every beat of the woman's heart. "Stay with me," I repeat, growing desperate.

Mickey is talking on the phone, giving our location. Declan is still standing behind me. "Put pressure on her wounds," I shout. "We have to stop the bleeding."

Declan doesn't move. He just stands there, shaking, as rain runs down his face.

Mickey is faring better and joins me on the ground. "Where?" she asks, then finds another wound on the woman's abdomen to press.

The pressure I'm putting onto the soaked bandage is barely stopping the flow of hot blood. I need to do more. I pull my hands away and whip my t-shirt over my head. Dressed only in my bra, I wad the shirt and press it to her chest. Rain slides down my bare skin. I shiver with fear and cold.

Mickey meets my eyes. Hers are wide with panic. "What else? What can we do?"

I try to remember my first aid training from girl scouts, but all I come up with is CPR. That's for someone not breathing. This woman has fallen unconscious, but her chest is rising and falling beneath my hands. Barely moving, but keeping her alive.

I think of Ford again, wondering what he'd do, but come up with nothing.

Then I think of God. "We pray and we wait for the ambulance."

As I pray, I press on her wound as hard as I can. I feel her blood drying on the backs of my hands. I feel my palms growing warm as her blood seeps through my shirt.

Her breathing slows even more, and sounds more like a gurgle than a breath.

"We're losing her," Mickey shouts.

Declan still hasn't moved. I look over my shoulder at him. His mouth hangs open slightly and he's breathing fast. "Can you lift her legs?" I ask.

He doesn't move right away. I pull one hand away from the soaked shirt and slap him on the shin.

"Her legs?" he asks in a daze.

"Lift them to keep the blood to her head. I don't know what else to do."

He finally moves, drops to his knees, and pulls the woman's legs onto his lap. "Like this?"

"That's good," I say. My nose is itching like crazy and I swipe at it. I feel a wetness warmer than the rain skim across my skin and realize I just spread blood on my face. I ignore that and look at the woman. Her face is streaked with blood, but I don't see any injuries there.

"What happened to her?" Mickey finally asks the question we are all thinking.

"Stabbed, if I had to guess," I say.

"But how did she get here?" Declan says in a soft voice.

The woman takes a gurgling breath and I think she's about

to speak. I lean closer to her, ready to hear anything she has to say.

She releases the breath in a rush.

And she doesn't take another one.

"No, come on, stay with us!" I shout.

A small way down the path, just beyond the red poppies, a familiar light opens in the night, an illuminated door that breaks the darkness.

The woman's spirit stands in front of the light, looking down on us.

"Don't go yet. Please. Stay here," I beg. "Come back."

Her eyes dart my way, and I know she hears me.

"Don't go," I cry, reaching my bloody hand for her.

She looks sadly at her body on the ground, then turns. She takes a step and the light closes around her.

"No!" I scream. "Come back."

I let go of the soaked shirt and pull the woman's head into my lap. "Come back," I cry.

She lies completely still in my grasp, her eyes open and staring blankly up at me.

I feel Mickey's hands on my bare shoulders. "She's gone, Rylan. We did all we could."

"I saw her cross over," I say shakily.

"I know," she drops to her knees and wraps me in a hug. She feels warm against my wet skin. I gently place the dead woman's head back on the path and collapse into Mickey's arms. She shakes next to me as we both cry in shock and sadness.

In the distance, sirens begin singing.

The ambulance is too late.

We hold each other like this for a few moments. Eventually, I pull away from my best friend and give her a weak smile, pulling myself together. Only then do I remember Declan.

He's still holding the woman's feet in his lap, his shoulders slumped and a look of total confusion on his face.

"You okay?" I ask, rubbing my bare arms and suddenly conscious I'm only wearing jeans and a bra.

"I-I don't know." He scoots away from the woman, rubbing his hands on his legs as if to brush them off. "What in the world just happened? Where did she come from?" He spins around, looking into the dark. "I don't understand."

I look past the garden, across the fields on two sides of the property, toward the woods behind. There are no lights from other houses close by.

The only lights I can see, besides the windows of the mansion, are the red and blue flashing of the ambulance tearing down the driveway.

"Help is here," Mickey says.

Standing, I look at the poor woman on the ground. "Too late for her," I say heavily. "I wish she'd talked to me."

The ambulance parks behind my Caddy, the EMTs rushing to us across the yard.

"She's gone," I say sadly when they reach us.

The EMTs don't give up so easily. They work on the inert body for several minutes before pronouncing her.

I pull Mickey away to a bench in the corner of the garden as they do their work. It's wet, but we sit anyway. Declan follows us, standing close by. "You okay?" I ask them both.

Mickey's teeth are chattering and rain drips on her face, but she nods.

"I don't understand," Declan repeats.

I scan the area, hoping against hope her spirit will come back and tell us what happened. I'm shivering and tingling, but I'm pretty sure that's from the cold, not a spirit.

"Did you see anything that would tell us what happened?" Mickey asks.

I shake my head. "She just looked at her body, then me,

then crossed into the light. She didn't say anything. I don't think she had time."

"You saw that?" Declan asks, his voice full of doubt. "How could you see that?"

I'm not in the mood for explanations of my abilities. We've been over it all before.

"It's what she does," Mickey comes to my defense. "She's seen it lots of times."

Declan chews on a thumbnail for a long moment. "You really see it all? It's not just for your show?" he finally asks, his accent heavy.

"You invited me here to find a ghost, but you still don't believe I can see them? What's the matter with you?"

He raises his hands in defeat. "I guess I wasn't sure. I've been hearing those things like I said and I figured…"

"You figured what?" a man says from the dark.

I turn around fast, relieved he's finally here.

Ford looks from my eyes to my chest, then back up to my eyes quickly. I'm suddenly very conscious of the fact that I'm only wearing my bra.

FOUR

FORD PIERCE

When I get the call to a stabbing at Krieger Mansion, my heart catches in my throat. I'm fairly sure Rylan is at the mansion tonight, helping Declan Rathborne with some kind of ghost problem.

If something has happened to her...

I drive fast, lights and sirens blaring all the way to the mansion. When I see Rylan's tan Cadillac in the driveway, the stone in my stomach grows. She's here somewhere.

She better be all right.

I sit in the car a moment, the rain pelting the windshield and the wipers frantically swiping. The ambulance is here too, which tells me the victim must not have made it. If there was a chance, the ambulance would be gone. A few squad cars have arrived before me, their lights swinging around the expansive property.

In the beam of my headlights I see Rylan and Mickey and Declan. They are huddled together, shivering in the rain. I am flooded with relief that she is safe.

With a start, I realize Rylan is not wearing a shirt.

I blink hard at that, then reach in the back seat for my extra jacket.

I climb out into the rain, jacket in hand, and approach the group.

Declan's South African accent carries across the dark yard.

"You really see it all? It's not just for your show?" he asks. I don't like his tone.

Rylan is perturbed at the question, her almost bare chest heaving.

"I guess I just figured..." Declan says.

"You figured what?" I interrupt, joining the group. Now that I'm close, my attention is grabbed by the expanse of bare, pale skin before me. Against my will, my eyes drop to the black bra and I pull them back to Rylan's face.

She has blood up her arms and a streak of it on her cheek that is smeared from the rain. Her hair is wet and clings to her shoulders.

"Ford," she breathes, making my stomach flip. "You're here."

"They called me," I say, feeling lame. "Here." I hand her the jacket.

She looks down at her bloodied arms. "I'll get it all dirty." She's shivering a little, water sliding down her skin.

"I don't mind." I put the blue jacket around her wet shoulders, fight the urge to wipe the blood off her cheek.

She slides her arms into my jacket and wraps it around her slim waist. I catch Declan watching her, appreciatively.

"Thank you," she says, a small quiver in her voice.

"You okay?" I ask. "All of you?" I look to Mickey, including her in the question.

Mickey just nods slightly. She looks pretty shaken up. She has blood on her hands and holds them away from her.

"That was intense," Declan says. I glance briefly at him, then turn my attention back to Rylan.

"We'll need a formal statement in a bit, but what happened?" I ask, leading the group under the front portico to get out of the rain.

"We were up in the turret." Rylan turns and points to the small rooms on each end of the roof. "We saw a shadow in the garden. When we came downstairs, we heard screaming, so we went to look." Her voice starts out shaky, but gains strength as she goes.

"You didn't think to just call us and stay inside?" I ask, rougher than I intended.

She lifts her chin. "She needed help."

"But there could have been anyone out here. Obviously, there's someone dangerous around or she wouldn't have been stabbed."

"We thought of that. We had knives."

"Knives?" I look to Mickey for help. "Really?"

"That's all there was," Mickey says miserably.

I shake my head at the three of them. "You could have gotten hurt."

"Well, we didn't. That poor woman did," Rylan snaps. This sobers me even more.

"Okay, so you came outside. What happened next?" I look toward the garden and the blue tarp they've put over the body.

"She was lying on the path and moaning. At first, there was so much blood, I didn't know where to put pressure, but I found a large wound on her chest." She pushes her wet hair off her face. "She had a bandage there," she adds.

"A bandage?"

She's warming to the idea. "Yeah. It had come loose. I pushed it down on the wound, but it was soaked. Eventually I used my shirt instead, but it didn't really help." Her voice sad and low.

"Rylan saw her cross over," Mickey says.

I raise my eyebrows. "You did?"

Rylan nods. "I tried to get her to stay." Mickey rubs Rylan's shoulder in comfort. "But she crossed over too fast. She didn't say anything and then she was gone."

I glance over my shoulder as a car pulls in. "There's Tyler," I say. "You guys stay here and we'll come back for your official statements."

"Can we go inside? It's getting cold out here," Declan asks.

"This whole area is a crime scene. You can't go inside," I tell him.

"My house too?" Declan balls his hands into fists. "We had nothing to do with this. All three of us were together."

"He's just doing his job," Rylan says, putting her bloody hand on his arm. Declan looks at the hand, then flinches away from her when he sees the blood.

I like the man even less in that moment.

I leave the three of them under the relative shelter of the portico and join Tyler as he walks toward the garden. I give him a quick rundown of what Rylan told me.

"And they have no idea where she came from?" Tyler looks down at the blue tarp. Red petals from the nearby poppies are scattered across the tarp, torn from their flowers by the rain and wind. In another place, they would look pretty.

"No idea. They didn't see her until she was in the garden."

Officer Frazier guards the scene. "Detectives," he greets us with a curt nod. "Glad you are here."

Tyler and I nod back. "What have we got?" Tyler asks.

"Stabbing victim. At least two wounds according to the EMTs." Frazier pulls the corner of the blue tarp up, showing us the body, but keeping her covered from the rain to preserve evidence. "Strange thing," he continues. "She has bandages. They've come loose, but she was patched up at one time."

"That's what Rylan said," I add thoughtfully, looking at the woman's pale, blood-streaked face.

"Rylan's here?" Frazier asks, looking across the yard toward the house.

"She and her friend, Mickey Ramirez, and the home owner, Declan Rathborne, found the woman and tried to save her," I say as I slide on latex gloves and hand a pair to Tyler.

"Was she filming that show of hers?" Frazier asks.

I stare at Frazier a beat, wondering at the edge in his tone. "I think so."

He shakes his head a little, but holds his tongue.

I turn my attention back to the woman. A shirt is balled up on the woman's chest. It was once light blue, but it's now nearly black with blood. "Whose shirt is this?" Tyler asks.

"Rylan's," I say.

I feel Tyler watching for my reaction, but I don't give him one. Instead, I return to my initial impressions of the victim.

"She's dressed in jeans and a t-shirt, so hopefully she wasn't assaulted. Marrero will have to confirm."

"Has he been called?" Tyler asks Frazier.

"Actually, he just pulled in," Frazier says.

The coroner's black van parks behind my cruiser. Marrero and a few of his team walk our way in yellow plastic ponchos. He's holding a bag in one hand and a clipboard in the other. The wind blows his hood off and his white comb-over flies askew in the wind. By the time he reaches us in the garden, his thin hair is sticking straight up. He drops his case and quickly smoothes the hair back into place and pulls his hood up.

He darts hard eyes my direction. I look at the ground, not wanting him to know I saw him in disarray. Marrero is hard enough to deal with, I don't need him to start this investigation off mad.

"What do we have?" he asks Tyler.

"Stabbing victim," Frazier says.

"Hmm," Marrero says, not looking at the victim yet. "Krieger Mansion. That writer lives here, doesn't he?"

"Declan Rathborne," I say, wondering if Marrero reads his books. I hate to admit I read his first one. It was okay. A bit graphic for my taste. I see enough in this job, I don't need to read about the bad things humans can do to each other.

"Right," Marrero nods and turns back to the victim under the tarp. He studies her for several moments without saying a thing. "Michelle," he suddenly snaps into the wind.

His assistant has been talking low with Tyler off to the side of the scene. She jumps and hurries over to Marrero. He hands her the clipboard and starts rattling off details for her to write down. Michelle scribbles as he describes the wounds. It is all medical jargon that I don't fully understand. Tyler is watching Michelle and I have to wave to catch his eye.

"Let's walk around while they do their preliminary," I say.

"Don't go too far, Detectives," Marrero barks.

"Yes, sir," I say and Tyler and I follow the path out of the garden.

The rain has let up to a slow drizzle but the moon is still hidden behind heavy clouds. The sudden storm has blown itself out. I turn on the flashlight on my phone and shine it on the ground.

"There won't be much of a blood trail after all this rain," Tyler says.

I know that, but I search anyway. "She came from some-where. She didn't just fall into the garden with the rain." I do a sweep of the entrances to the garden, hoping to find a drop of blood or something to tell us where she came from, but find nothing but wet grass and a few stray leaves.

"What are we going to do with Rylan and Mickey and that Rathborne guy?" Tyler asks when we see them under the covered entry. Mickey and Rylan are huddled together and look cold even from across the yard.

"We can let them go and get their statements after we're

done here," I say. "We have to check out the mansion and the outbuildings. It will take a while."

Tyler nods and we make our way across the wet grass to the front of the house.

Rylan has the jacket I gave her wrapped around both her and Mickey. Only then do I notice Mickey is only wearing a t-shirt and is shivering, too. Rathborne leans against the front door, his legs crossed at the ankle. He stands up straight as we approach.

"What did you find out?" Rylan asks. I focus on her face, not on the skin I can see through the opening of the jacket.

"Nothing we can share," I say. "We're going to cut you all loose and get your statements later. But first. Was there anyone else here tonight?"

"Just us," Declan says.

"No staff or anything? This is a big house."

"Anita the housekeeper is out for the night and so is Keith the groundskeeper."

"Both are out? Like together?"

"Not together." Declan makes a sound of disgust. "Just out. I sent them away so we could do this," he points to Rylan, "without any distractions."

"You mean you didn't want them to know you think the house is haunted."

"Look, can I go in now?" Declan asks.

"No. The house is part of a crime scene."

"So I have to leave? You still think I'm part of this?"

"We can't rule anything out," Tyler says.

"Can I at least get my dog? Evie has been inside all this time."

"You can get your dog. Rylan, can you guys get a ride back to Ashby?"

She chews on her lower lip for a moment, then says, "I can call Aunt Val to come get us."

"I'd call Marco, but he's at work," Mickey says.

"I guess I could call my Uncle Sawyer," Declan says, searching his pockets for his phone.

"Val can probably take us all back to town and drop us off," Rylan holds her phone to her ear.

Michelle, the CSI tech, joins us under the portico. "Detectives, Marrero's ready for you," she smiles shyly at Tyler.

I raise my eyebrows in question to Rylan. She's talking to Val on the phone, but gives me a conspiratorial smile. She caught the undertones between Tyler and Michelle too.

"We'll be in touch," I say to the group and head back to the garden. I feel eyes on my back. When I look back, none of the group is watching me. Is there an unseen set of eyes somewhere in the dark?

FIVE

RYLAN FLYNN

I pull Ford's jacket tighter around my shoulders as I watch him walk away out of the very corner of my eye so he can't see. Aunt Val has agreed to come pick us up.

All three of us.

"Where can we drop you off?" I ask Declan. "A hotel or a friend's?"

"Probably my Uncle Sawyer's. I'll have to call him. But I left my phone in the house. Wonder if I can go get it."

"I don't think so," Mickey says.

He looks to me. "Can I borrow yours?"

"Don't make him drive all the way out here, just ride with us," I find myself saying.

Officer Frazier steps under the overhang, startling us. "Rylan, Mickey," he greets us formally. "In trouble again, I see."

After everything we've been through tonight, I'm not in the mood for attitude from little Jimmy Frazier.

"We didn't do anything. We tried to save her," I point out.

He tucks his thumbs into the armholes of his vest. "Okay. Sure." He turns his attention to Declan. "I'm here to escort you in to get your dog."

"Can I get my camera too?" Mickey asks. "I left it in the turret when we saw the woman's shadow."

Frazier thinks a moment. "Were you filming?"

"Yes."

"Then it could be evidence."

"I wasn't filming out the window. I was filming Rylan."

"Still. There might be something on the tape."

Mickey is not pleased to be losing her camera, but she doesn't press the issue.

From inside the mansion, Evie begins barking. "I need to get her. She's probably freaking out from all the people here," Declan says. "Can I open the door?" he asks sarcastically.

Frazier takes his thumbs out of his vest. "Be my guest."

Declan just blinks at him, perturbed, then opens the door.

Evie bolts out, barking so hard at Frazier her body bounces off the paving stones.

"Nice dog," Frazier says, backing away.

"She won't hurt you. She just thinks she's big," Declan says, scooping Evie up and holding her against his chest. She finally stops barking. "Can I get my phone, too?"

"Sorry. It's evidence now." Frazier doesn't sound sorry. "This whole property is a crime scene."

"I have nothing to do with this." Declan motions to the garden, stepping closer to Frazier.

"We'll see," Frazier says tightly.

I look from man to man, the air fairly tingling with tension.

Evie whines and squirms. Declan loosens his grip on her.

"When can he get his phone?" I ask, trying to defuse the situation.

"When they are done searching the house. That could take a while."

"So tomorrow?" I ask.

Frazier sticks his thumbs back into the arms of his vest, puffs his chest out. "Maybe tomorrow. You have the dog now, you should leave."

"We're waiting on my aunt. She's going to give us a ride."

Frazier's eyes land on my jacket, and he sees the insignia on the chest that says Ashby Police. "Where'd you get that jacket?"

"Ford loaned it to me."

Frazier seems even more perturbed than usual. "That's police issue. You shouldn't wear it."

"I don't have a shirt on," I tell him boldly. Something in his expression tells me he already knew that. "You want me to take it off?" I begin opening the jacket.

He has the decency to look away. "No. Keep it. Just make sure Detective Pierce gets it back."

I wrap the entirely too large jacket around my waist again, confused by Frazier as usual.

"I'm sure they will want your formal statements tomorrow," he says, pulling his thumbs back out of his vest. "Looks like your ride is here." With that, he turns and walks away.

When I look down the tree-lined lane, I see Aunt Val's SUV parking behind the cruisers.

"Let's get out of here," Mickey says. "I'm freezing and I want to go home." She sounds shook up.

"Hope Uncle Sawyer is still awake," Declan says, shifting Evie in his arms.

I lead the three of us through the maze of cruisers and official vehicles to Val's dark blue Suburban. She is standing next to it, searching for us.

"Rylan, are you okay?" she asks, hurrying to take me into her arms. I allow her to hold me, but keep my bloodstained hands away from her.

"I'm fine," I lie. I put on a brave face for her, but inside I'm shaking.

Val rubs Mickey's arm in a soothing gesture, but she's looking at Declan. "Declan, good to see you again." Her tone says there's nothing good about it. Val helped me through the break up with Declan and knows it wasn't easy even though it was my choice. She knows all about how he didn't believe in my gift and how that caused a rift that I couldn't get over. In true Val fashion, she took my side and defends me fiercely.

"Hello," Declan says, not meeting her eyes but looking down at Evie. I wonder if he has seen her at the donut shop. Somehow, I can't picture Declan getting his fingers sticky with frosting.

"Can we go?" Mickey says, rubbing at the goosebumps on her arms. "I just want to go home."

Val leads us to her SUV and Mickey and I climb into the back seat. Declan hesitates, then takes the front seat. He places Evie on his lap.

"Your dog is cute," Val says, trying for polite.

"Thanks," Declan says awkwardly. "Her name is Evie."

If I wasn't so upset, I'd laugh at how Val is making him squirm. After all we've been through together tonight, I again find myself taking pity on him.

"Do you have a new book coming out soon?" I ask the first thing that pops into my mind.

He looks over his shoulder, animation in his eyes. "Not until September, but I'm really excited about it."

"I read one of them once," Mickey offers. I'm surprised. She never told me she read a book written by my ex. "Well, actually more than one. They're good." She darts a look at me and mouths *"sorry."*

Mickey can read whatever she wants. Still, it stings just a little.

Val catches my eye in the rearview mirror and I shrug.

"So, where am I dropping you?" Val asks Declan to change the subject. He gives the neighborhood of his Uncle Sawyer. We went to dinner there once, and I remember his uncle as a nice man. Quiet and curious. He was very interested in what I do, although at the time we were just starting to put the show together and didn't have much of a following yet.

We ride on in silence until we reach Sawyer's house. Headlights glare on the front door, the last of the rain misting in the beams.

"I probably should have called him first," Declan says, climbing out with Evie. "I hope he's up."

The front door opens and Sawyer looks out with concern, his shock of white hair bright in the headlights. "Can I help you?" he calls, holding his hand up to block the light. "Who's there?"

"It's Declan," he calls back.

Sawyer steps out onto the front step, wearing nothing but shorts and a t-shirt. "Declan, what happened? Are you okay?"

When he steps out, Aunt Val gives a little gasp of surprise. "That's his uncle?" she asks me.

"Yeah, Sawyer Lambert. His mom's brother. Why?"

"No reason." She puts the SUV into reverse even though Declan hasn't closed the door yet.

He turns quickly and shuts the door as we move backward.

The tires don't squeal as we leave, but almost.

SIX

RYLAN FLYNN

Mickey and I exchange a look with raised eyebrows. "Val, you okay?" I ask as we careen down the street.

"Why do you ask?" She meets my eyes in the rearview again.

"Because you pulled out of there like we were being chased."

"No I didn't. I just want to get you guys home and get back to George."

Val's dog is no doubt fine, so I wonder why she is lying to me. At least she has let off the gas a little so I don't worry we'll slam into anything. "Do you know Sawyer?"

She swallows instead of answering right away. After a few beats of listening to the wipers squeak, she says, "I did. Very well. But that was a long time ago."

I sit forward, pushing my head between the front seats. "And you didn't know he was Declan's uncle the whole time we were dating?"

"No. Look I don't want to talk about it." She pushes her bangs out of her eyes nervously.

I suppose if she wants to keep her secret that's her right, so I sink back into my seat. But my mind reels with how she could know Sawyer. I've never known Val to date anyone. Dad once told me she had her heart broken when her boyfriend died just after high school and never recovered. Was Sawyer a secret she kept from all of us?

I close my eyes and lean my head back on the head rest, pondering. I wrap Ford's jacket around me. Maybe a secret love isn't such a far-out idea.

A few minutes of quiet later, we pull up to Mickey's house. The place is dark, Marco still on his night shift.

Mickey hesitates, her hand on the door handle. "I guess this is me," she says weakly, making no move to climb out.

"You going to be okay by yourself? I can come in." What I really want is to go home, take a hot shower and fall into my own bed, but I'll go in with her if she wants.

"No. I'll be fine." She still hasn't opened the door. "She's okay, right?" she finally asks.

"Who?"

"The woman in the garden. You said you saw her cross over. She went into the light, right? Like into the good side?"

"As far as I know," I answer gently.

She nods and says, "Good. After what she went through, she deserves some peace." She pulls the door handle and hurries from the SUV. I watch her run through the mist to her front door. We wait until she gets inside and turns on a light.

"Ready?" Val asks.

"Hold on." I jump out, then climb into the front seat. I check the house again and more lights are on. Looks like Mickey has turned on lights in every room. "You think I should go in with her?"

Val looks pointedly at the blood still dried on my hands. "Maybe you need each other tonight. Or maybe you need some time alone, to think about what happened."

I rub my hands together. "I just want to shower and wash this off."

"I understand. I'll take you home." Val puts the SUV in reverse and we leave Mickey alone with all her lights.

"You haven't told me how you got all that blood on you."

At her words, I feel the heat of the woman's life pulsing out between my fingers. I look out the window. "It was awful," I whisper.

Val reaches over and pats my shoulder. "I can imagine." Something in her tone tells me she really does understand.

I turn to face her. "What happened to you?"

"That was a long time ago."

"So? It's obviously stuck with you."

"That's a story for another time." We are in my driveway now. "Do you want me to come in with you?"

I panic at the thought of her or anyone coming into my house. "No," I assure her. "I'll be just fine." I lean over and give her a quick hug, careful not to touch her with my hands.

"By the way," she says as I open the door, "nice jacket."

I smile for the first time tonight. "It is, isn't it?" With that, I jump from the SUV and hurry to my front door. I stand outside on the small porch and wave goodbye. Once she drives away and can no longer see, I walk around the house to the back patio door. Earlier today, the pile of boxes by the front door toppled over and I didn't have a chance to clear them.

The dining room by the sliding back door isn't much clearer, the table buried under clothes and books and who knows what.

The house has really gotten out of control. I stand and stare into the dark, over the odd furniture pieces, the boxes from Amazon that I haven't even opened. The collections press on me, but they also give me comfort. I step deeper into the house, following the path I've maintained to the front door. The pile of boxes leans against the door. I should clear the door, it's not safe.

I grab the top box, but before I can put it down, I have to look inside. Faces stare up at me through the dim light. The package is filled with cute farm animal figurines. For a moment, I forget about blood and spirits crossing. I touch the face of a piglet with a bow and smile. I bought this collection mostly for the pig. I take it out of the box and hold it to my chest.

Suddenly, emotions overwhelm me and my chest burns. "She died in my arms," I tell the pig, my eyes burning.

The pig keeps on smiling. A harsh difference from the pain I feel.

"Rylan, is that you?" Mom calls from her room.

I drop the pig figurine back into the box with the other farm animals, feeling guilty. I wipe at my wet cheeks. "I'm home," I call across the piles, down the hall.

"Did you eat?" The question she has asked me all her life and even now in death.

I didn't eat, but thoughts of food are far away.

"I'm good," I say as I duck into her room. The ghost of my murdered mother sits on her bed as usual, running her brush over the hole behind her ear. She studies me with concern. "You have blood on your face. What happened?" She places the brush on the bed and reaches for me. I want nothing more than to collapse in her arms, let her rub my back and tell me it will all be okay. That is not possible.

I settle for dropping to my knees next to the bed and leaning against the blankets. "Mickey and I went to do a filming for the show," I start, my voice small and tears streaming again. "We saw a woman in the garden. When we went to see what was going on, she was stabbed." I push my hair away from my face.

"Oh, how horrible," she gasps. "Is she okay?"

"No." I sniffle. "She died while I tried to save her." My voice breaks and I lower my face to the blankets, wishing more than anything that she could touch me.

"Oh, Rylan, how awful. I'm so sorry. What happened?"

"No one knows for sure but she was murdered."

"Murdered?" Mom says quietly, too thoughtfully. I think of the hole in her head and her own murder. I hope she isn't thinking the same thing.

I want to tell her how I saw the woman cross over. I want to try to explain how badly it hurt that I couldn't keep her on this side of the light. But I don't talk about crossing over to Mom. I can't bear the thought of coming home one day and finding that she has moved on herself.

Noticing a small smear of blood on the red-checked quilt, I pull away from the bed. "I need a shower."

"You are a bit bloody." She says it like I come home covered in blood all the time. She's already lost interest. Alive, she would have stayed up all night comforting me. In death, she has a very short attention span. I try not to take it personally, but tonight her vagueness stings.

"Good night, Mom," I say at the door.

"Did you eat?" she asks again, brush back in her hand. I stare at her a moment, sad beyond belief. I like to pretend she's the same as she was before. Times like this, it hits me.

She's really gone.

I don't answer, I just close her door.

I slide past the boxes piled in front of the door to my brother Keaton's childhood room. I'm thankful the thing on the other side of the door is quiet and lets me pass in peace. I'm not sure I have it in me to face its howling tonight.

I grab some cleanish clothes off the floor in my room and can finally take a shower. My reflection in the bathroom mirror startles me. My face has dark red smears from where I wiped at my tears. My eyes are also red and puffy. My hair is a tangled, damp mess.

I run the water in the sink while I wait for the shower to warm up. The water turns pink when I put my hands under the stream. I scrub them together hard, needing the sticky blood to go away.

The blood has stained the creases of my fingernails. I pump more hand soap and scrub at them. "Get off me," I beg the stains. They fade, but a faint imprint of red outlines all my nails.

I hope it will come off in the shower.

I almost hate to take off Ford's jacket. It smells vaguely of his cologne. I press the collar to my nose and inhale deeply. I imagine him here, telling me it will be okay.

You should tell him how you feel.

This is not the first time I've had the thought, but it is strong tonight, insistent.

The idea of saying the words to Ford in real life makes my stomach quiver.

I hurry and pull the jacket away. A woman died tonight, I should not be thinking of romance. Disgusted with myself, I climb into the shower and scrub hard with a wash cloth. The water finally turns from pink to clear, but I stay under the spray.

The poor woman in the garden will never again enjoy a hot shower. Nor will my mom. My chest hurts at the thought, but I keep the tears away until I lie down in bed. I wrap my arms around Darby, the giant bear that I found in a yard sale, and bury my face into his fluff that smells like baby powder and vanilla. I replace Mom's hugs with his.

Only then do I let myself break.

Images of the woman flood my mind. Memories of her hot blood make me cry out. Her face just before she crossed over haunts me. Sobs rack my body, making me shake.

Darby's arm rubs across my back.

I stop breathing for a moment. Did I just imagine he moved?

I sit up and look at the bear. His permanent smile seems a little crooked through my tears.

Surely I imagined the movement. I lie back down, but keep

the bear on the other side of the bed. My sobs have subsided now and I can clearly hear the thing in Keaton's room begin wailing.

"Not tonight," I beg the dark. "Please, go away."

It wails louder, bangs on the door.

I've had enough for one night.

Bounding out of bed, I prepare for a fight. I storm down the hall to the pile of boxes guarding the door and begin tearing down the wall I built.

Behind the door, the thing laughs and howls.

I toss boxes down the hall, heedless of anything that might break in them. Finally, the door to Keaton's room is no longer blocked. The door shakes as the thing inside pounds against it.

"Go away!" I scream at the door. "Get out of my house."

The pounding stops, but the laughter carries on.

I reach for the handle, ready to face it after years of hiding.

A different pounding echoes through the house. I turn my head to listen.

Someone is at my front door. I drop my hand from where it almost touched the handle.

SEVEN

MICKEY RAMIREZ

I flip on every light in the house when I get home. I use the hem of my damp t-shirt so I don't get blood from my hands on all the switches. The light does little to dispel the darkness in my soul.

She died. She actually died while I had my hands on her.

I look at her blood staining my skin. Some of it has smeared off from the rain, but there is still a lot of red on me. I hurry to the kitchen and turn on the faucet. The hot water rushes over my hands and I rub them frantically.

My hands are clean, but my arms still have spatter on them.

I need a shower.

First, I need Marco. I need to hear his voice.

Now that my hands are somewhat clean I can use my phone. My fingers are shaking so badly, I have trouble pulling up his number. I finally give up and just say, "SIRI call Marco."

A few moments later, he answers. "Is everything okay?" he asks as a greeting. I rarely call him when he's at work cleaning the middle school. I'm sure seeing my name on his phone has him worried.

"I'm fine. Well, not fine, but not hurt," I stammer.

"Mickey, you're not making sense," he says gently. "Just take a deep breath and tell me what's wrong." I sink into his reassuring voice and feel my heart slowing.

"We were at the mansion doing the show and we found a woman in the garden," I start. The memories crash back into my head as I tell the story. "She was hurt, bad. Stabbed I think."

"Oh no," he breathes. "Mick, oh man. Is she okay?"

"No. No she died." My voice breaks. "She died while we tried to save her."

"Wow, I don't know what to say. I'm so sorry, babe."

I lean my head against the fridge, wishing it was his broad chest, wishing he was here with me and not running a mop.

The fridge's compressor suddenly kicks on. I jump and make a startled noise.

"What was that?" he asks, full of concern.

"Nothing. The fridge turned on. Marco, I'm scared. I mean really scared."

"I know, I know. Look, I only have an hour left on my shift. I'll be home real soon."

The metal door of the fridge is cool under my forehead. I imagine his arms around me, his hands on my back.

"Tell me everything is going to be alright."

"You'll be fine. Better than fine. Where is Rylan?"

"She went home."

"She left you alone after what you went through?" His voice rises in concern. "Of course she did."

"Don't be mad at Rylan. This wasn't her fault."

"You were there because of her, because of the show. You should have been home safe and sound."

"I wanted to go. I like the show."

He takes a deep breath. "I know. I'm sorry. I just hate to think what you had to see tonight."

"Just come home soon. I'm going to take a shower and wait for you in bed."

"I'll be there just as soon as I can. I love you."

"I love you, too." I wait until he hangs up, then put the phone on the counter. My mouth is dry, so I grab a glass from the cabinet and turn the sink back on. As I fill the glass, I stare at my reflection in the window. My hair is damp and frizzing in a wild mess around my head. My face has a small smear of blood just below my eye. I wipe the blood away, scrubbing hard, frantic to get it off me.

I check my reflection in the glass. Something moves in the dark beyond.

Or behind me.

I spin, wondering if it's the ghost that Rylan sometimes senses.

The kitchen is still.

When I look back out the window, I see the movement is from outside in the dark.

I press my face close to the glass to see. Beyond the grill on the back patio, a shape definitely shifts.

My blood runs cold and I jerk away from the window, feeling exposed.

Is someone out there?

I think of the emails hidden on my computer. *"I'm watching you."* I look again.

The area around the grill is empty now.

"You're imagining things," I say out loud. "There's nothing there."

I down the glass of water and stare out the window. I still feel exposed. If there was someone out there, they can easily see me.

Stepping away from the window I flip off the kitchen light. Then I go through the house and turn off all the lights. I check all the locks on the doors.

"Marco will be home soon," I tell myself to calm my nerves. I want to call him again, to tell him what I thought I saw, but I don't want to worry him with my paranoia. "Just shower and go to bed."

Before I head to the bathroom, I look out the kitchen window one more time. The hydrangea bush near the grill is blowing in the wind.

"Just the bush," I say with relief. "Now stop being silly."

Still, once I get upstairs, I snap the blinds down in the bathroom and pull the curtain closed over the small window.

It's not until the hot water has soaked some of the tension from me that it dawns on me. The hydrangea is on the right of the grill. The shadow I saw was to the left. There really was somebody out there.

EIGHT

RYLAN FLYNN

The thing behind Keaton's door slams into the plank between us, making it rattle.

At the front door, someone bangs again.

I look down the dark hall at the boxes tossed all over. I grab the closest and put it in front of Keaton's door. I move another one and another until I have a pile blocking the door again, then I climb over the others to make my way down the hall.

"Rylan? Are you in there?" It's my dad. I hear the front doorknob rattle. Thankfully I locked the door. Dad has not been in this house since he and Mom divorced several years ago. At that time, it was clear and clean. He'd be appalled if he saw the state it's in now.

No one is allowed to see. No one must ever know.

I walk along the path I've cleared to the garage and open the overhead door. The garage is full of boxes from my apartment that I never unpacked, but at least it is an organized mess.

Dad waits for the door to open, his feet shuffling in the growing gap. When the door opens enough to see his face, he immediately looks relieved to see me.

"I've been calling you for over an hour," he says instead of hello.

I reach for my phone in my pocket only to find it's not there. I must have left it in my bedroom. "I turned the ringer off when we started filming earlier. I'm sorry."

"Keaton said you had a bad night. That a woman died in your arms. He was worried about you."

I wonder for a minute how my brother knows about the dead woman already, but then I figure he must have been alerted by his office at the District Attorney's.

"Did he land the case?" I ask.

"He was called to the scene to look it over. He's there now or he would have come himself." Dad looks over the stacks of boxes.

"So he's at the mansion?"

"Yeah. When he got there, Ford told him about your involvement so Keaton called me."

"But I'm fine."

Dad eyes me critically. "Are you? You look a little shook up."

I roll one of the charms of my bracelet in my fingers. The cross one, my favorite. "I'm fine," I say without much conviction.

Dad hears the weakness in my voice and pulls me into his arms. It's been a long time since Dad has held me like this. I melt into the protection of his arms and let the façade down. I'd wanted to collapse like this with Mom. Dad is here, he's real.

"You don't have to be strong all the time," he says. "Ever since you got your gift, after that accident, you've seen a lot. It's bound to make an impression."

"I haven't thought about the accident in years," I say, pulling away and wiping at my sniffling nose.

"I think about it a lot. We almost lost you to that pond."

At his words I can feel the painfully cold water engulfing

me as I fall through the ice. My fingers push against the frozen surface, unable to find the hole I fell through. My lungs begin to burn, then to scream. I need air, but there is none.

And then the light.

The beautiful light that opens before me.

I want so much to go to the light, but something pulls me back. Pulls me from the water onto the snowy surface.

Dad hovers over me, beating on my chest.

And I take a breath.

I nearly drowned that day, and nothing's been the same since.

I push the memory away, deeply buried where I always keep it.

"I don't want to think about it," I say, shaking my head.

"Of course, you've had enough tonight." He wipes his face and I wonder if it is rain or tears. He looks at the stacks of boxes again. "What's all this?" He changes the subject.

"It's stuff from my apartment that I never moved into the house." I hope he doesn't ask any more questions. I don't really have a good reason for the boxes out here, except that it didn't take long or too many garage sales to fill the house after I inherited it when Mom was murdered. There was never a good time to unpack the boxes. Mom's house was already fully furnished, so I didn't need anything.

"If you ever need help moving this stuff in, you know you only have to ask."

"I know. Honestly, it's fine." I don't want to talk about my stuff. I don't want to talk at all. I yawn loudly, hoping Dad will take the hint.

"I should probably get going," he says. "If you're really okay. I can stay and we can talk it out if you like."

I shake my head, maybe a little too vigorously. "No. I just want to sleep."

"I understand." He looks thoughtfully at the boxes then at

me. His intuition is clearly telling him that something's up. Thankfully, he lets the matter drop.

"I appreciate you coming to check on me. It means a lot."

"Anything for my girl," he says and drops a quick kiss on my cheek. "Call if you need anything."

"I will," I say and watch him walk to his car. The night has grown chill after the rain and I'm wearing only a t-shirt and shorts. I shiver. It makes me think of icy water again.

I watch Dad drive away into the night and turn to go back inside.

A shadow catches my eye in the corner of the garage.

I look to the ceiling. "Please. No more tonight," I beg God.

A rustle shakes behind the boxes, followed by a meow.

There's a cat in my garage.

I walk around the pile and peer between the boxes and the wall. Green eyes in a black face look back.

"Hey there," I say gently. The cat takes a cautious step closer, but stays in the crack behind the boxes. "Where did you come from?" The cat blinks in response.

I put out my hand for it to sniff and get a half-hearted hiss.

"Yeah, I'm not in a good mood either," I tell it. I stare at the cat a few moments, wondering what to do now that it's in my garage. I need to shut the door, but I can't lock it inside.

"You hungry?" I finally ask. I sound like my mom. The cat takes another step toward me. "I'll be right back."

I hurry into the house, down the path to the kitchen. I'm pretty sure I have a can of cooked chicken somewhere, a left-over from when Mom was alive. I dig through the cupboards until I find it. Opening it, I toss the lid toward the trash. I miss, but I don't pick it up.

Instead, I go back to the garage, hoping the cat hasn't left.

The garage is quiet, and when I look behind the boxes there is nothing but shadows.

The cat is gone.

I stand alone with an open can of cooked chicken in my hand.

A darkness fills my soul. A loneliness, an ache. The events of the night crash into me.

I sit the chicken just outside the door, in case the cat comes back, then I hit the button. The door shuts behind me, loud in the quiet of the night.

Scooting past Mom's door and Keaton's, I climb back into bed. Darby smiles at me and I swear his head turns.

Holding him at arm's length, I place him in the hall then return to bed.

Curled under the pile of blankets, my mind fills with thoughts.

Where did the stabbed woman come from and why was she bandaged?

Did she walk over through the woods? Did someone drop her on the road? Why stab her then try to heal her?

Just before I drift off to sleep, I do what I usually do, think of Ford. This time I say a prayer that he's finding out what happened to the woman I watched die.

NINE

FORD PIERCE

Thankfully, the rain has let up to barely a damp mist, but any hope of following blood that the victim might have left has long since washed away. It took everyone available, but we have searched the mansion from top to bottom. We found no sign of where the victim might have come from.

Just an overly pretentious house for one man. The kitchen alone is about the size of my place, not to mention the floors of rooms that I doubt Declan Rathborne sets foot in.

As the night wears on, we finish our search of the out-buildings. There are several barns full of undisturbed dust and obviously not used. There's also a carriage house filled with expensive cars. We search each car, but find nothing of note.

The last place we search is the caretaker's cottage just inside the woods.

Nothing. Not a thing that would lead us to believe the victim came from there.

Discouraged, I look to Tyler. He has a shadow of a beard by this time of night and looks as haggard as I feel. I rub my chin and find it is also stubbly.

"Any ideas?" I ask.

He gazes across the property. "I've got nothing. It's like she just dropped from the sky into the garden. Did Rylan or the others say anything at all about the direction she came from?"

"No. We can ask again when we do the official statements in the morning, but I doubt they will be much help."

Looking into the dark, a few lights shimmer through the mist. "There are some farms that way," I point out. "Maybe she came from one of them."

"Or the woods," Tyler adds. "Do we know what's on the other side of the woods here? Isn't it that big pig farm?"

"Yeah, I think it is. Maybe she trekked through the trees and wound up here. We'll have to check it out."

I glance toward the groundskeeper's cottage. "And talk to the caretaker and housemaid. It's a long shot, but maybe they saw something before they left."

I spot Keaton Flynn in the garden. When he feels me watching him, he comes over. "Any luck?" he asks.

"Nothing to report to the DA," I say stiffly, not ready to give any kind of statement. It's always a bit weird working a scene with Keaton. He's been my best friend since we were kids. We played on the same baseball and wrestling teams, and I spent weeks in the summer with him at his aunt's house. We used to go on double dates together. He's a great guy.

Working a scene with him watching over our shoulder is an entirely different matter. One I'm not completely comfortable with yet. I hate having to tell him we didn't find anything useful.

"Well, she came from somewhere," he points out uselessly. This doesn't help my frustration and I'm itching to get to that pig farm.

"We can't make evidence appear," I grumble. "Maybe she was dropped off on the road. This is fairly remote. She could have been dumped and headed toward the lights of the mansion."

"We're not done looking," Tyler says. "We still have to canvas the area, as remote as it is."

"Sounds good," Keaton offers. "I think I'm all wrapped up here for now." He looks at Rylan's car in the front parking area, behind the crime scene tape. He shakes his head a little in disgust. "Leave it to my sister to get herself wrapped up in this."

I feel the need to defend her. "She was just in the wrong place at the wrong time."

"That happens to her a lot lately."

"She's been a big help," Tyler says, surprising me.

"I just don't want her hurt." Keaton looks me full in the eye. "She's been through enough."

"She can look after herself," I say.

"Can she?" he counters. "We both know Rylan can be a bit impulsive, and that can be dangerous."

I clench my jaw. Tonight was just a fluke of luck that she was involved, but I've voluntarily let her into investigations before. She's come out okay, but she has been in danger, I can't deny that.

"She's home safe now," Tyler says, trying to soothe the building tension.

"I sent Dad to check on her," Keaton says. "Maybe he can talk some sense into her and she'll stay out of this one." He doesn't sound like he believes his own words. He takes a deep breath and lets it out. "Anyway, enough about Rylan. I've officially been assigned this case, so keep me informed."

"Of course," I say, wishing we had more to give him.

He looks toward the Krieger Mansion then back at me. "Declan Rathborne. Again. Just great," he says then walks away.

"So he doesn't like this Rathborne guy either," Tyler says.

"He used to date Rylan a few years ago. When Margie Flynn was murdered, he couldn't take it and they broke up. At least, that's what Keaton said. I don't think he likes the man much."

"I take it that's the general consensus?"

"Look at this place. What kind of man needs a home like this?"

"A successful one, I guess."

"An ostentatious one," I counter.

"Jealous?" he asks. Sometimes I hate the way Tyler can see through me.

"No," I lie. "Now let's go talk to the people that live by that light over there."

Tyler smiles and shakes his head. "When will you learn?"

I catch sight of Michelle, the crime scene tech. She's watching us. "When will you learn?" I ask him, motioning to her. She sees me and turns away.

"What?" he fakes, smiling wide. "She's cute."

"That's true," I say. "When are you going to finally ask her out?"

"I've only seen her at scenes. It hasn't been the right time."

"You wait for 'the right time,' you'll be waiting forever." I push him gently in her direction. "Marrero left a while ago. Now is good."

He doesn't resist, just puts his shoulders back and walks toward Michelle. She pretends not to watch him. I turn away to give him some privacy.

It crosses my mind to wonder what would happen if I asked Rylan out.

I shove that idea away quickly. She's Keaton's little sister, nothing more.

I almost believe it.

TEN

RYLAN FLYNN

Mickey looks pale and pinched when she picks me up. Ford called and said my car had been cleared and I could get it this morning. Aunt Val is working at the donut shop so I asked Mickey to drive me.

I suppose I could have asked Declan, as the house has also been cleared. I assume his uncle will drive him home and I could have bummed a ride with them.

I'd much rather see Mickey and check how she's doing.

Judging by her expression, she didn't fare too well last night. I wonder if I look as shaken as she does.

"Hey," I say tentatively as I climb into her car, Ford's jacket in hand. She meets my eyes and I see an intensity there. "What's up?" I ask, afraid of the answer.

She looks away and I buckle in. "I don't think I can do this anymore," she blurts, her voice shaking.

"Do what?" I play dumb.

"This." She points from me to her. My blood goes cold.

"Be friends?"

"Be partners. I can't keep chasing after ghosts and getting into situations like last night."

I stare at her in surprise. I never thought I'd hear those words from her. From my best friend. "This doesn't sound like you. You love doing the show. Besides, last night was not because of the show."

"I was there because of the show. I could have been home safe and sound."

"Is this coming from Marco?"

She flips her eyes at me then back to the road. "No," she says unconvincingly. "This is coming from me. It's just—" She stops suddenly, then changes tactics. "You wouldn't understand."

I don't know what to say. The quiet of the car is like a canyon between us.

"You're just shook up. It will pass."

We are at a stop sign and she turns in her seat. "Will it? A woman died, Rylan. Dead. Gone. Crossed over. And we were there." She holds up her hand. "I had her blood all over me."

Adrenaline pumps through me, a fear unlike facing a ghost, more important. I can't lose Mickey.

"I'm so sorry," I say lamely. "I wish I could take it all back, for both of us. But you have to know we were there for a reason. God chose us to be with her at the end."

"You sound like your dad."

"Well, Dad is often right. God has a plan."

"That's the easy way out. If you're right and God has a plan, I think his plan for me is not to do the show anymore."

"Mickey, you can't be serious." I start to panic. "I need you."

"You'll still have me, as a friend, but I can't be your cameraperson anymore."

"You know you're way more than a cameraman. I can't do the show without you."

She keeps both hands tight on the steering wheel, won't look at me. "I just can't. At least for a while."

I hear the crack in her armor and I calm a little. She'll come around, she has to. "We can take a break and see how things go," I offer.

Mickey thinks a long moment. "A break?"

"We're both pretty raw from last night. We do important work. We have to remember that."

"You do important work. I just tape it."

"You know it's more than that. You run the whole business."

"Marco got a raise last month. I don't have to do the show to pay the bills. I could get a job as a custodian at the school with him if it came to that."

"You don't want to be a custodian. That's great for him, but it's not what you want."

"What I want is to not be surrounded by death all the time." Her voice has risen.

I don't have a response. I've never looked at what we do quite like that. We drive in silence and soon the Krieger Mansion looms into view. Yellow tape surrounds the garden, but otherwise you'd never know something horrible happened here last night. The property is so lovely in the late morning light I can't imagine that it was the site of a grisly death.

Mickey parks behind my Cadillac. "Do you think Declan is home?" she asks. "He was cleared, right?"

"Ford said the house was clear. I don't know about Declan himself."

She whips her face in my direction. "You think they're looking at him as a suspect? He was with us the whole time."

"I know that and I know him. There's no way he was involved. I'm just not sure what the police think."

Mickey shakes her head and her dark curls bounce. "Marco was right."

"About what?"

"You've changed. It's not your fault. With everything you've been through, you've gotten hard. Before, you'd never think that Declan had anything to do with the murder."

"I didn't say he did." I'm starting to get mad now. "I said the police might think he did. Not me. That's not fair."

Mickey takes a big breath and lets it out slowly. "Maybe a break will be good for us."

The words are like a slap. "A break from the show, sure. Not a break from us."

"That's what I meant. A break from the show." She puts the car in drive. "You have your keys?" Not subtle at all.

I shake the keys in my hand. "Got them. Look, Mickey—"

"Marco is waiting. Plus, I have to go to meet with Ford later to give my official statement. I should be going."

There's nothing else to say, so I climb out of the car with Ford's jacket. The door is barely closed when she pulls away.

I'm alone in front of the imposing house.

Only then do I realize my back is tingling.

I turn slowly, not wanting to startle whatever spirit is close. A figure stands in the window by the front door. It's a Black woman wearing a black dress. The same woman we saw last night.

She stares right at me. I raise my hand in greeting. She doesn't respond, doesn't move.

The front door flies open and the woman disappears.

"Holy flip, you scared me," I say to Declan as he steps out into the sunlight.

"I thought I heard a car out here. I was afraid it was the police coming to take me in."

"The police aren't going to do that. I've come for my car. I guess I should have called and told you I was coming."

He looks down the long lane leading to his house. "Who dropped you off?"

"Mickey."

"Oh," he says awkwardly. Neither of us knows what to say. Is there a protocol for talking to your ex-boyfriend the night after you both watched a woman die?

Luckily Evie bounds out the door. "Hey, girl," I say to the dog, bending to pet her, happy for the distraction.

"It's weird being back here after," Declan says, his accent thicker than usual. "I don't understand how that poor woman got here."

I stop petting the dog and look toward the garden and the yellow tape. "Me either. Did the police tell you anything?"

"They'd tell you before they'd tell me," he says pointedly, looking at the jacket in my hand.

"They only said the house and cars were cleared and I could come get the Caddy."

"You should see the house. They made a mess. Not sure what they thought they'd find."

"Yeah." I don't know what else to say. I really just want to go. After my discussion with Mickey, I want to be alone to think over what she said. No more *Beyond the Dead*? I can't even fathom it.

"Look, I need to get going," I say and take a step toward my car.

"You don't want to come in?" He sounds so hopeful. "I... I don't like being here alone right now. It's creepy."

"Maybe you should stay at your uncle's."

"I don't want to put him out." He gives me a sheepish grin, the one that used to do me in.

"You could stay at a hotel."

"I might." He shrugs.

Tires on gravel crunch behind me. For a crazy moment, I hope it is Mickey coming back to tell me she was wrong and the show's back on.

It's a rusting blue flatbed pickup truck.

"That's Keith, the groundskeeper. He was out of town last night. He doesn't know what happened here yet."

A burly man with a full dark beard cranes his neck to look at the yellow tape. He parks the truck and jumps out. "What is up with that?" he asks Declan, his long beard blowing in the breeze.

"I'm going to go." I hurry to my car before Declan can stop me. I nod to Keith as I pass him. He nods back, his face full of questions.

As I start the car, I look toward the window near the door again. The woman is there, watching me.

I wave and she waves back.

ELEVEN

RYLAN FLYNN

Normally, I'm excited to see Ford. This morning, I'd rather be anywhere than sitting in a hard chair near his desk giving my formal statement about what happened last night. I don't want to relive it. It's been playing over and over in my head and that's bad enough. I don't want to say the words.

But the woman deserves to have her story told, and it's my turn.

Gripping his dark blue jacket on my lap, I muddle through my description of last night's events, leaving no detail out. I even tell them about seeing her cross over, how bright the light was, how sad her face was.

When I finish, Ford and Tyler look at me seriously. "You saw her go?" Tyler asks.

"Unfortunately." I run a finger along the zipper of the jacket.

"And she didn't say anything?" Tyler pushes.

"If she had, I would have told you." I'm tired and frustrated and snappier than I should be. "Look," I add contritely. "I would love it if I had any information that would help, but I don't. She just appeared out of nowhere. At least that's what it looked like to us up in the turret."

Ford looks thoughtful. "Did you see any cars in the area at that time? You can see pretty far from way up there."

I think about it a moment before I answer, wanting to be sure to get it right. "I didn't. We were pretty focused on the house and looking for ghosts."

"Did you see any?" Tyler asks, a little too excited. "Any ghosts?"

I think of the woman I saw in the window this morning. "Just for a moment."

Ford eyes me skeptically. "What does that mean exactly?"

"We saw a female spirit just before we saw the woman in the garden. I saw her again at the window at Declan's this morning. She's very old, probably 1800s, judging by her dress."

Ford sits back in his chair, his blue eyes boring into me. "Another witness."

For the first time since we found the dying woman, I feel some hope. "Right. Maybe she saw something we missed."

"So you'll do it?" Ford asks, still studying me.

"If it will help find who hurt that woman, I'll do anything I can. Did you find out her name yet?"

Ford looks away and I know he has. "I can't say."

"You can't even tell me her name?" I look to my hands, the nails still stained with the woman's blood. I tuck my hands away under Ford's jacket.

"We will make the official announcement later today," Tyler says. "So when do you want to do this visit with the ghost?" he changes the subject back.

"We'll have to ask Declan first. It's his house," I say.

Now both Ford and Tyler stare at me with that intense cop glare. It makes me squirm. "How well do you know this Declan Rathborne?" Tyler asks.

I flick my eyes to Ford, not sure how much he knows about our history together. "We used to date a few years ago."

Judging by their expressions, they already knew that part. "And you broke up why?" Tyler pushes.

I dare another quick look to Ford. He seems interested in my response. "We had some differences of opinion."

"Most couples do," Tyler says. "Care to elaborate?"

I grip the jacket in my lap again and take a deep breath. I haven't told anyone the true reason we broke up. Him not believing in my gift was only part of it.

"He thought I had something to do with my mother's murder."

Ford leans toward me. "That's ridiculous."

"Is it?" I ask miserably. All the pain and doubts of that time come rushing back. "I was supposed to be with her that night. I canceled at the last minute and she was alone."

"You did not hurt her," Ford says. "Or want her hurt."

"But I went with Mickey to do a filming. We were just starting the show and we had a last-minute call. I chose work over Mom and she ended up dead."

"You not being there may have saved your life. The killer may have taken you both," Ford says, his face so close I can the see heavy stubble on his chin. His eyes hold mine for a long moment and I feel like I'm falling.

"Why did Declan think you had anything to do with what happened?" Tyler asks. "That's a bit of a jump."

"Because when we got to the location for the filming there was no one there. It was a set up. Declan once said it was a bit too convenient. He swore he didn't mean it, but I could never forget he said the words. So that was the end."

"Why have we never heard about this part of the story? It's not in the file they had at the time."

"It's not? I told the police that night."

"I've read the file a few times. The part about you being called out on a bogus claim is not in there."

I chew my lip a moment. "Why wouldn't it be there? Detective Holtzberry took the statement himself." My voice is rising in agitation. "Did he leave it out on purpose?"

"He wouldn't do that," Tyler protests. "Might be it got overlooked. Things like that can happen unfortunately."

"Is the rest of my statement there?"

"I'll have to look to be sure nothing else is missing," Ford says.

"Can you ask Holtzberry about it?"

"He died," Tyler says solemnly. "He had a heart attack about a year ago."

"So you got the case," I finish for him. "And nothing has progressed on it since." I try not to sound bitter. I know these two have done everything they could. With no leads from forensics or witnesses, or any tips, Mom's case went cold very fast.

"We've done all we can," Ford says evenly.

"I know that," I drop my eyes. "But this is new."

"This is new. And we will definitely look into it, but I don't want you to get your hopes up," Ford says. "The missing statement might not mean a thing."

We sit in the quiet for a few moments while I stare at the insignia of Ashby Police Department on the front of Ford's jacket. It suddenly dawns on me I should hand it to him. "Oh yeah, here's your jacket. I washed it."

He hesitates a beat, then takes the jacket back, his fingers just barely brushing against mine.

"Thanks for loaning it to me." My cheeks burn at the memory of being mostly undressed in front of him. He's seen me in a bikini lots of times, in the summers he'd spend with Keaton when we were kids, but that was a long time ago.

"My pleasure," he says, then lays the jacket on the back of

his chair. "So, back to the ghost hunt, we'll ask Declan about it when he comes for his statement today."

"Have Mickey come, too," Tyler adds.

"I can't do that," I say miserably. "She's taking a break."

"Break from what?" Ford asks gently.

"She said from the show. But I think it's from me." The words hurt more than I thought they would.

TWELVE

FORD PIERCE

Tyler and I spend most of the day recanvassing any homes even remotely close to the Krieger Mansion. It is tiring and frustrating work. House after house of no one seeing anything starts to wear on a person.

We go house by house in order of proximity to Krieger Mansion. My shoulders are tense by the time we pull into Speckler Farms, the pig farm directly through the woods from the mansion. I try not to get too excited. I feel like we might be onto something with this one.

We pull down the long lane, pastures of pigs on either side. These pigs are fuzzier than usual and have large floppy ears.

"KuneKune pigs," Tyler says, seeing me peering out the window at the unusual pigs. "Gourmet pork."

"How do you know so much about pigs?"

"I know lots of things about lots of things," he says with a smile. "I'm an interesting person."

"Sure you are. Just park already."

He pulls the cruiser next to a red pickup truck near a barn and we climb out. The pigs run up to the fence, curious about the visitors. "See, friendly animals," Tyler says, reaching over the fence to pet a few fuzzy heads.

I pass on petting the pigs and look around the farm. There doesn't seem to be anyone around, not even a dog barking at our arrival.

"Think anyone's home?" I ask.

We listen to the farm and a rhythmic thudding comes from behind the barn. Tyler leaves the pigs and walks around the red and white building with me. As we grow closer, the sound becomes unmistakable. Someone is chopping wood.

We turn the corner and a man swings an ax into a log. The log flies into two pieces. He picks up the largest of the pieces and places it back on the chopping block. He raises the ax again, oblivious of our presence.

"Mr. Speckler?" I ask just before he drops the ax.

He chops the wood without looking up at us. "Yeah. What do you want?" he asks as the pieces fly.

I hold out my badge. "We're Detectives Pierce and Spencer. We'd like to ask you a few questions."

Speckler picks up another chuck of wood and puts it on the chopping block, ax still in hand.

"Do you mind putting the ax down?" Tyler asks, stepping forward.

Speckler finally looks at us, then drops the ax with an exaggerated motion. "Better?"

"Thank you," I say. "If you don't mind, we'd like to ask you about last night. Were you home?"

"Is this about that woman that died over at the fancy pants mansion?"

"Yes," I say. "Do you know anything about it?"

"Only what everyone knows. That some lady got herself stabbed and died over there."

"Were you home?" Tyler repeats.

"I was. But I don't know anything. Krieger is quite a ways from here. Even with binoculars, I couldn't see anything that happened there. Too much woods in the way."

"So you've tried looking at the mansion with binoculars?" I ask.

"No," he sneers. "I just mean no one could see anything happening there from here. I was home, but I was in bed. Chores start early here, so I'm usually in bed early."

"Those are some nice pigs," Tyler says, trying to form a bond of some sort. "KuneKune, right?"

Speckler seems surprised. "Yeah, that's right." He softens. "You know pigs?"

"Not really. I just heard about that kind on a show once. They have those little things hanging from their chins. They're cute."

"Waddles." Speckler's chest puffs out as if he's talking about his children. "They are wonderful pigs. Make the best pork."

"I bet," I say, ready to change the subject from pigs back to the case. "Have you ever been to the Krieger Mansion?"

Speckler looks at the ground. "No. I mean I've driven by it, but I've never been in the house." He rubs at his right hand and I notice a large scrape.

"What did you do to your hand?"

He looks at the hand as if he didn't realize it was injured. "This? I caught it on a fence. It's nothing."

"Doesn't look like nothing," I press.

"Look, this wood isn't going to split itself. Unless you have anything else, I'd like to get back to work," Speckler says, picking up a chunk of wood that had fallen off the chopping block.

We won't be getting any more from the man, so we walk back around the barn to the car.

"Well, we're back where we started, nowhere," I say after closing the door and starting the car.

"We ruled a few things out," Tyler says, always the optimist.

"Hopefully, the ghost at the mansion saw something useful." I don't know if I'm more excited about a possible witness or that I get to see Rylan again.

THIRTEEN

RYLAN FLYNN

The Krieger Mansion looks even more intimidating tonight than it did last night. The sun is long gone and there are few lights on inside. The two turrets seem to scrape the moonlit clouds.

Ford's black Malibu is parked out front. He and Tyler are inside the car, waiting for me, their silhouettes dark against the front entry lights.

I wish desperately that Mickey was with me. Not because I need her camera skills, but because I could use the reinforcement of my best friend when dealing with both Declan and Ford, and even Tyler with his open curiosity about my gift.

"Holy flip, stop being such a baby," I grumble and force myself to climb out of the car.

The heady scent of lilacs from the garden hangs heavy in the chill night air. I breathe deeply and close my eyes to savor the scent. I make a mental note I should plant some lilacs in the backyard at home.

Unless I find some at a garage sale, I doubt I ever will.

"Ready?" Ford asks as he climbs out of his car, shaking me out of my moment of quiet.

"Just smelling the flowers," I say.

"Oh yeah, I hadn't noticed. They smell good," he says a bit awkwardly. I wonder if he's as nervous as I am. The entry light is behind him so I can't see his face clearly.

"Are you getting anything yet?" Tyler asks over the top of the Malibu.

I take a moment to gauge my body's reaction to the house. My belly is a little fluttery, but I attribute that to nerves. "I don't think so. I may not be able to find the woman again. I barely saw her last night and I only got a glance of her this morning as I was leaving."

"I'm sure you'll be fine," Ford says and leads me to the front door.

The door is made of thick, dark wood with wavy, leaded windows in them. Behind the door there's a scratching noise and then barking.

I smile. "Looks like Evie knows we're here."

"Is she big?" Tyler asks, a little worried.

I laugh out loud. "She's a tiny chihuahua. Don't worry, I'll protect you."

Tyler shakes his head at me. "I think I can manage."

Ford knocks on the door regardless of Evie's barking. The door opens immediately.

Declan glances at the two men then his eyes land on me. "Hey," he says. "Back again?" He's obviously trying to make a small joke, but it lands flat.

"I appreciate you allowing us to do this," I tell him, brushing my hair back over my shoulder.

"If it will help find out what happened to that woman, I'm all in," he says. He steps back into the entryway to let us in.

Evie has stopped barking and stands behind his ankles, growling low.

"Cute dog," Ford says. I can't tell if he's being sarcastic or not.

"Don't mind her. She just thinks she's tough." Declan bends to pick her up, and settles her on his arm.

We all stand, looking at the dog for a long silent moment.

"So. How does this work?" Declan finally breaks the awkwardness.

"I think we'll do like we started last night. Let's walk around the house and see what I see."

"But you saw something here this morning?" he asks.

"I saw a Black woman looking out that window. She was wearing old clothes, like from the 1800s. A dark dress."

The three men look at the window as if the woman will suddenly appear. "She's not here now?" Ford asks.

"I don't see her. I'm not really getting any tingles or anything either," I say with regret.

Declan looks skeptical and Evie whines.

"I guess we walk around and see what happens," I say. "Shall we start at the top and work our way down?" I want to go back to the turret, see if being there brings any scrap of memory back from last night.

"Sounds good," Declan says and leads us up the stairs. He turns on lights as we make our way through the house. The fixtures are old and aren't particularly bright. Each one creates a small island of illumination as we go. We walk from each island to the next, up stairs, down halls and to the door leading to the turret.

No one says anything as we creak along the wooden floors. It feels strange to be doing this without Mickey and her camera. Normally, I'd be talking, narrating what we are doing for the video. No need for that tonight.

As we make our way down the third-floor hall, a door suddenly opens and a woman looks out, her face pinched with irritation. She looks directly at me.

"Hello," I say.

She shakes her head in disgust and closes the door.

"Who's that?" Ford asks.

"That's Anita. She's not happy you're here. She thinks this whole haunted business is ridiculous."

Ford looks at Tyler, then says, "We thought she was out of town. When we called, she said she was at her sister's and wouldn't be back until tomorrow."

Declan shrugs. "She got back about an hour ago. She was so shook up about the murder she went straight to her room."

I don't want to talk about the rude housekeeper. I'm anxious to go back to the turret, hoping against hope that I'll see the ghost from this morning and she might know something about what happened. Maybe she was looking out a window and saw where the woman came from.

The narrow turret door is closed. Before I open it, I do another mental check of sensations in my body. Still nothing. I'm beginning to wonder if I really saw the woman. Then I remember how I felt when I first entered the mansion last night. The pressure in my back was so heavy it nearly knocked the air out of me. There is something here.

I reach for the handle and pull the door. It pushes open and cool air rushes down the stairs.

"That's strange," Ford says. "Why is it so cold? It's pretty warm up here on the third floor."

We all exchange looks then hurry up the dark stairs. Ford takes the lead, followed by Tyler. I go next.

Evie growls and barks twice at the stairs.

"Maybe I better stay down here with her," Declan says, so we leave him in the hall.

The chill breeze grows stronger as we climb the stairs.

"How did that happen?" Ford asks in awe.

When I reach the top of the steps, I see what has Ford so confused. Every window in the small round room is broken, and broken glass covers the wood floor, sparkling in the moonlight.

In the middle of the room, under a pile of glass, lies Mickey's camera where she dropped it last night. It has been smashed as well.

"Not Mickey's camera!" I exclaim. "What happened?" No matter how startled Mickey was last night, I know she didn't smash the camera like that when she put it down.

"This was definitely not like this last night," Ford says. He turns on his flashlight and shines it around the room that barely holds the three of us. Tyler turns his on too and looks out on the roof.

"All the glass is inside," he says. "How is that even possible?"

Ford and I look out as well. There isn't a sliver of glass on the shingles.

"It's like they all blew in at once. That storm we had wasn't strong enough to do this," Ford says.

"This place has been here for nearly two hundred years. We've certainly had worse storms in that time," I say, pulling my head back into the room. The breeze blowing through the broken windows is cool and goosebumps dot my arms. I rub at them, noticing the smell of lilacs on the breeze. I step from the window and glass crunches under my Chuck Taylors.

"Everything okay up there?" Declan calls up the stairs.

Ford and Tyler exchange a look I don't want to decipher.

"All the windows are broken," Ford calls down. "Do you know anything about it? Did you hear glass breaking earlier?"

"I haven't heard anything. Of course, I spent a long time in my office writing. I listen to loud music when I work. Wait, all the windows are broken?"

"All of them," Tyler says.

Declan stomps up the steps and Evie whines in complaint, sensing his tension. There isn't room for him to come all the way up, so he stops a few steps down, his head just above the floor.

"Wow, what a mess! What happened?"

No one has an answer. We stand quietly, the only sound the wind whistling down the steps into the house.

"Mickey's camera is smashed, too," I say after a while, bending to pick it up. The large lens is broken and hangs at an odd angle. "Guess it's a good thing she's taking a break. This obviously doesn't work anymore."

"Did someone throw rocks at the windows or something?" Declan asks.

"There aren't any rocks up here. Just glass. It looks like they all blew in at the same time."

"That's not even possible," Declan says. "Wait, let's check the other turret." He disappears down the steps.

We follow him through the house, me carrying Mickey's broken camera. When we reach the door, we all hesitate in the island of a nearby light. As we grow closer to the door, my back begins to sizzle.

Ford reaches for the handle and pulls. The door won't open.

"Is this one locked?" he asks Declan.

"I hope not because I don't have a key."

Ford turns the handle and pulls again. The handle will turn, but the door is stuck closed.

FOURTEEN

RYLAN FLYNN

"Now what?" I ask, staring at the stuck door, my hand on my back to soothe the tingle.

"We don't really need to go up there," Tyler says. He glances over his shoulder down the hall into the gloom.

"I'd like to see if this turret is all broken up too," Ford says. "You sure you don't have a key to this door?"

"I don't. It can't be locked anyway, the knob is turning. Maybe the wood is swollen from last night's rain," Declan says.

"Maybe," Ford concedes and lets go of the useless handle. He turns his attention to me and the reason we are here. "Are you getting any sensations or seeing anything?"

"Yeah, something strong, but I don't see anyone."

Ford glances around like he'll see whatever I'm feeling. He looks disappointed that it's just us in the hall.

"I'd really hoped to talk to another witness. Maybe the woman you saw has some information that would be helpful to the case."

"I'm sorry. If she's here, she isn't showing herself." I hate that I've let them down, but I don't control the spirits.

"Maybe we should just get back to work," Tyler says, a little jumpy.

Evie squirms to get down, so Declan places her on the floor. She runs off with a clicking of her claws on the wood floor. I watch her go. Even she doesn't have faith that I'll find something useful.

"We could check out the rest of the house," I offer. "She might still make an appearance," I say hopefully. "If that's okay with you," I add to Declan.

"You can do whatever you need," he assures.

Ford and Tyler have lost their enthusiasm for the project but dutifully follow me through the rest of the mansion. I wander around, Mickey's camera cradled against my chest, feeling like a failure. The strong tingle I felt fades as we look.

We eventually reach the front door again with nothing else of note. There's not even a hum left from the sensation I had earlier.

"I'm really sorry for wasting your time," I tell them. "I swear there was something here. Right by this window."

"I'm sure there was," Ford says. "Whatever it was is gone now."

"What about the turret windows?" Declan says. "What happened there?"

Blank faces all around. "No idea," I finally say. "The wind?"

Declan seems unconvinced. "Whatever it was, I'll have to have Keith fix those windows."

"Keith Gillespie, the groundskeeper?" Ford asks. "He's back?"

"Got back this morning."

"Great, we can talk to him too and this trip won't be a waste," Tyler says.

That stings.

"Again, I'm really sorry," I say.

"Don't worry," Ford says with a hard look at Tyler. "We

know you can't control the ghosts. If she doesn't want to talk, she won't."

I appreciate the words, but I still feel bad.

We stand awkwardly in the expansive entry to the mansion. "Well," Ford says, "thanks again, Rathborne." He holds his hand out to shake. "I'm sure we will be in touch," he adds with a touch of warning. Declan takes his hand and shakes it harder than necessary. A tension fills the entryway.

"Let's go talk to Keith Gillespie," Tyler says, stepping toward the door and turning the knob.

Ford lets go of Declan. "Thanks for your help," he says to me. "Sorry she didn't show up for us." He sounds sincerely remorseful.

"I don't know what happened." I feel the need to explain.

"Don't worry about it." He looks like he wants to say more, but instead he follows Tyler outside.

Leaving me alone with Declan.

"Well, thanks," I say, edging toward the door. "Sorry we put you out for nothing."

"It was interesting," he says, his accent a little heavier than before.

I let the silence sit for a moment, then ask, "You really have no idea where the woman came from last night?"

He seems surprised by the question. "I was with you and Mickey. I only know what you said you saw and then..." He lets the words trail off.

"That was intense, wasn't it?" I rub a hand down my jeans as if it is dirty. "I don't think I will ever get the feel of her blood off of me."

He nods thoughtfully, his hands perfectly clean, my nails still stained.

"Well, I should go," I say and step out under the overhang. The night is cool, the scent of the lilacs strong. Ford's car is still here, so I assume he is talking to Keith Gillespie. I'm almost jealous they have something to do. I want to help with the investigation, but my only possible contribution just failed.

I place Mickey's broken camera on the front seat next to me, then start the car. I look back toward the mansion as I drive away, hoping to see the woman in the window again.

The house is lit up from the many lights we turned on as we looked for a spirit to talk to, but there are no shadows at the windows. "Where are you?" I whisper, then turn my attention back to the driveway, sad and full of failure.

FIFTEEN

FORD PIERCE

I'd really hoped for more from our adventure with Rylan. The broken windows are curious, but they don't help determine what happened here last night. Maybe the groundskeeper will have some insight.

Tyler and I walk across the yard to Keith Gillespie's cottage. It is a small home with a creaky front step. A light is on inside and a shadow moves across the window when we knock.

The green-painted door swings in and a man with a full dark beard looks out curiously. He has the dazed look and slightly pink face of someone we woke up. The smell of fish pours out the door.

"Can I help you?" he asks, on guard, rubbing his hand down his long, full beard.

I hold out my badge and so does Tyler. "We are Detectives Pierce and Spencer. We'd like to ask you about last night."

Gillespie blocks the opening of the door with his body. "I wasn't here. I was on Lake Michigan fishing for walleye. Got myself a nice mess of them."

"We know you weren't here. We searched your cabin last night," I tell him.

"Declan told me. You sure left a mess here."

"Sorry about that," I say. "Sometimes the techs get a little overzealous."

"Is that what you call it?" Gillespie gripes.

"Just doing our jobs," Tyler says. "Can we come in and ask you a few questions?"

Gillespie finally steps back and lets us in. I'd rather not return to the cabin. The small space is full of taxidermy animals. Several deer heads with wide racks, a raccoon and a beaver. Even a small bear, obviously killed as a cub. I'm not much of a hunter and the display makes my stomach turn. On the small counter by the sink are the remains of the walleye he mentioned. A bucket on the floor holds the guts, judging by the flies and the stench. I turn away.

"Not sure what you thought you'd find here last night," he says. "I had nothing to do with that woman dying in the garden. Like I said, I wasn't even here." He offers seats at the small square table just off the kitchenette. Tyler takes a seat. I'm too keyed up to sit. Instead, I pace the dark blue and green braided rug that dominates the room, trying not to notice all the glass eyes watching me.

"Have you seen anything of note lately? Suspicious activity of any sort?" I ask.

"No. And nothing happens around here that I don't know about. I can see most of the property from that window there." He sits on the rumpled couch.

I look out the window and he's right. Past a few trees, I can see the back of the house, the garden, the carriage house, all of it.

"I keep a close eye on things for Mr. Rathborne. That's part of my job. Unofficial, of course."

"Have you worked for Rathborne long?" I ask, finally taking a seat on a straight back chair.

"Since he bought the mansion. He kind of got me with the

purchase. I've been working here for twenty years. My grandpa worked here before that. Caring for Krieger has been in the family for decades," he says with obvious pride.

"Do you like working for him? Is he good to you?" I ask.

Gillespie's eyes narrow. "How do you mean?"

"Do you have any problems with him? Does he cause trouble?"

"He mostly stays inside and out of my way. He writes a lot in his office. Sometimes I see his light on late into the night. Once in a while he sits in the garden thinking and taking notes. I suppose he won't want to sit there anymore after what happened."

"So no complaints?" Tyler asks.

"What are you getting at? You can't possibly think he had anything to do with this. He is the artistic type. Not the type to get his hands dirty, if you know what I mean. Soft. He might write about murder, but he would never be part of it."

"People can deceive," I say, leaning back in the hard seat.

Gillespie shrugs. "Maybe. But I don't see it. Once, we had a mole problem in the yard. They were tearing up the ground with their tunnels something fierce. I set traps to catch them. I'd get one and shoot it. Declan found out and made me stop. He said that was animal cruelty. He'd rather have the mole problem than see me shoot them. That doesn't sound like a ruthless killer to me."

"And you would know about killing," I say, motioning to the dead bear cub standing on its hind legs.

"That was different."

"I'm sure it was."

"I wasn't even here and Declan didn't do it. Besides, he was with that ghost hunter and her friend at the time. That's a pretty good alibi."

I can't disagree, but I don't want to talk about Declan anymore.

"What about the housekeeper, Anita Monroe?"

"What about her?" The small amount of skin showing above his beard turns pink. I wonder if there is more going on with Anita than just working for Declan.

"Could she have hurt the woman?"

"Anita couldn't hurt a fly. In fact she doesn't even squash spiders. She makes me come gather them and let them loose outside."

"And you don't mind helping her, I gather," Tyler says.

Gillespie shifts in his seat. "I don't mind. She's a nice lady."

I try to picture this burly man releasing spiders outside and can't quite see it. He probably smashes them once out of Anita's sight.

I sense we won't get any more from Gillespie, so I walk to the door.

Tyler stands too and hands the man a business card. "If you think of anything at all that might be helpful, give us a call."

Gillespie looks at the card then sits it on the tiny square table next to an overflowing ashtray. "I don't know what I might have to say. You're barking up the wrong tree here. No one here at Krieger hurt that lady. Maybe her old man did it and dumped her out front. Sometimes people drop unwanted kittens off here."

"And what do you do with the kittens?" I ask, looking around as if a stuffed kitten will be on display.

Gillespie looks disgusted. "What do you think I do with them? I take them to the animal shelter," he says stiffly.

"Just call if you think of anything," Tyler says and opens the door.

Gillespie doesn't see us out onto the front steps. He just shuts the door behind us with a mumbled, "I will."

The night sounds from the woods are loud. Bugs and frogs sing. The moon is high and the night is lovely. It's hard to imagine that just last night a woman lost her life a short distance from this spot.

The lights are on in the carriage house used as a garage, and the sound of a trunk slamming closed carries across the yard. The light flips off and a dark figure scurries toward the house. It looks like a woman carrying a bag.

"Anita Monroe?" I call into the dark.

She stops and turns to face us. I can barely make out her expression in the dark, a mixture of surprise and irritation.

"Detectives, done with your ghost hunt?" she asks a bit sarcastically.

"For now," Tyler says. "I was curious, do you believe the mansion is haunted?"

"Of course not." She shifts the plastic bag from one hand to the other. "Or course, Mr. Rathborne does. At least I got a night to stay with my sister out of the deal."

"We know you weren't here, but have you seen anything suspicious in the past few days? Has Rathborne been acting differently or anything?" I ask.

She makes a sound of derision. "Mr. Rathborne? You think he's involved in this? That's a hoot."

"Is it? A woman died here on the property."

"Look around you, there are plenty of places to hide a person. The woods, the other farms. There's even an abandoned barn just up the road from here."

"If you had to guess, what do you think happened?" Tyler asks.

She moves the bag to her other hand again. "I honestly have no idea. I can tell you it's pretty scary."

"So scary you're out here alone in the dark?" I point out.

She smiles slowly. "I needed protection."

"What kind of protection?" Tyler asks.

Anita holds the bag up. "This little baby."

"What's in the bag?" I demand, my instincts on high. Tyler goes stiff too.

She notices our change in mood. "Nothing too exciting. Just my pepper spray."

"Can you please drop the bag?" I ask sternly.

She drops the bag on the grass. I take out my flashlight and shine it inside. There's a package of pepper spray, unopened.

"I picked it up at the store after I got your call yesterday. It's not illegal is it? This is a big house and after what happened..."

I return the bag to her. "It's not illegal."

"I forgot it in my car. That's what I'm doing out here."

"Thank you for your help," Tyler says. As he did with Gillespie, he hands her a card. "Call us if you think of anything that might help the case."

Anita glances at the card then slides it into her pocket. "I will, of course. Good night, Detectives."

We watch until she lets herself inside the mansion, then walk in silence across the yard back to my car.

"Well, this was a bust," Tyler says once we're driving away. "No ghost and no one knows anything."

He's right and it's making me grumpy. "We must be missing something," I say. "She didn't just appear out of nowhere."

Tyler's phone chirps that he has a text. Mine does too at the same time. Since I'm driving he checks his.

"We got the confirmation from Marrero. It is confirmed the woman is Skylar Chrisman from Fort Wayne. So did she run to Ashby and ended up in that garden?"

"Or was she nabbed in Fort Wayne and taken here? Maybe Gillespie is right and her man roughed her up then dumped her."

"While she was still alive?"

We drive the back roads to town, both lost in thought. "Skylar Chrisman, what happened to you?" I say to myself.

SIXTEEN

VALERIE FLYNN

I've had this idea for a long time. Ever since Rylan told me she could talk to ghosts when she was in middle school, I've wanted to ask her a favor. It's a big favor, one I can't ask lightly.

After seeing her covered in blood, it brought it all back.

I was once covered like that too.

Then seeing Sawyer again, after all these years, seemed like a sign.

It is time to ask Rylan to find him. I know Justin is out there. At least his spirit. I think Rylan senses it too. For twenty-five years I've yearned to talk to him again.

With Rylan's help, maybe I can.

I sit on the porch, watching the moon rise above the trees, my phone in my lap. I lift it several times, my fingers aching to call her.

Several times, I lower it. My nerve lost.

George presses against my legs, sensing my agitation.

"I know, boy. I'm being a wimp."

Still, I don't call. I stare at the shadows in the trees beyond the clearing, wondering if Justin is out there.

A shadow shifts between two trees. Was that him or just a cloud in front of the moon?

"Stop being a baby."

I lift the phone and press the button that will call Rylan. It's kind of late and I wonder if she's even up.

She answers on the second ring. "Aunt Val, man am I glad to hear from you. I've had the worst day," she says.

I'm taken aback. I don't want to add to whatever is wrong.

"What happened?"

"First Mickey quit the show," she says in a rush. "Then I had to give my official statement down at the precinct. This morning I thought I saw a ghost at the mansion and Ford and Tyler wanted me to talk to her. So we went to Declan's again and tried to find her. We didn't see her, though. I didn't see anything." She ends her story with a sigh of disappointment.

"I'm so sorry," I hedge. Should I even ask her tonight? I've waited for years, I can keep waiting.

"Phew," Rylan says. "I feel better now that I dumped all that out." She takes a breath. "So what's up? It is late for you to be calling."

She waits a beat, but continues before I can form an answer. "Wait, is everything okay?"

"Yes, yes, I'm fine. Everyone is fine."

"Good. Except you don't sound fine. Not really."

There's a question in her words.

"Well, I wondered if you could come over," I say before I lose my nerve. "I have a favor to ask."

"Of course," she says quickly. "I'm on my way back from the Krieger Mansion so I'm sort of close. I'll be right over."

"Thank you, Rylan."

"Seriously, is everything okay?"

"Hopefully, it will be. I'll explain when you get here." I hang up the phone and put it back in my lap. As I wait for

Rylan, I keep checking the shadows. "Justin, are you out there?" I call into the wind. I listen and scan the dark, but all I hear are the frogs from a nearby pond. "She's coming to find you. Please be out there," I beg.

SEVENTEEN

RYLAN FLYNN

Shadows stretch across the lane leading to Aunt Val's cabin, plunging it into darkness. The trees are so close together moonlight barely touches the gravel. The beams from my headlights cut through the gloom and soon shine on Val sitting on her porch.

She raises a hand in greeting.

My curiosity grows. It is pushing midnight, so why is Aunt Val even up, let alone asking me to come over?

I turn off the car and the clearing grows dark, lit only by the moon. I step up to the porch and George bounds to me, eager for a pet. I scratch him behind the ears and study Val. She seems unhurt, just a little tense.

"Hey." I try for casual. "You're up late." Normally, Val is up at 5 a.m. to open the donut shop, so she goes to bed early.

"I have the morning off." She shifts in her chair, crosses one leg over the other, then drops it back.

I take my usual spot in one of the three rocking chairs. We sit in silence for a while, me dying of curiosity, her rubbing her hands on her pants and not looking at me.

Finally, I can't take it anymore. "Want to tell me what's going on?" I ask gently, bracing myself for the worst.

She dares a look at me, then turns her eyes back to the woods.

"Do you believe in soul mates?"

I'm not sure what I expected her to say, but this isn't it. I think of Ford and how I hope he might see me differently, when the time is right. "I suppose I do."

She pushes her bangs out of her face and says, "I had a soul mate."

"You did?" I ask gently.

"Back in high school. His name is Justin Beckley." She takes a deep breath and lets it out. "He died many years ago."

I have heard the short version of the story from Dad over the years. He said losing Justin is why Aunt Val never married. "Dad told me once."

She looks at me in surprise, then softens. "I suppose everyone knows, really. It was a big deal when he was killed."

"How did it happen?"

She pushes the chair and it rocks slowly. "That's the story I want to tell you."

"I'm listening." I can't believe we are having this conversation. Aunt Val is not one to share her feelings, especially not such personal ones.

"It involves Declan's uncle, Sawyer Lambert."

"Okay," I lead her gently.

"Justin and I started dating junior year. Sawyer was his best friend, and we spent so much time together Sawyer became a good friend to me, too. The three of us got up to all kinds of fun. Just regular kid stuff." She rubs George's head as she talks. "Justin and I were so close. I truly thought we were going to be together forever. There was talk of a ring in the future, but we were so young at the time." She closes her eyes and leans her head back on the chair. "Those were the best days of my life, those days with Justin."

I don't say anything, afraid to break the spell. I just roll the charms on my bracelet, especially the dog one that Ford gave me years ago.

"Those days weren't meant to last, I guess," she continues. "They ended abruptly one night when we were out with Sawyer." She stops talking, rubs her hands down her thighs again as if they were dirty.

After a long time, I ask, "What happened?"

"One night we went to a concert in Fort Wayne, the three of us, then we drove home together. We were almost back to town when a car crossed over the center line and hit us." Her voice sounds far away, lost in memory. "Justin was driving and the car slammed into his side of the car. We spun around and around down the road and eventually came to a stop on the edge of a ditch."

"That's awful," I exclaim.

"I was so scared, I think I screamed the whole time. I know I hit my head on the dash and it kind of knocked me out. When I woke up, Sawyer was leaning in the passenger door, shaking me. 'You have to get out of here, the car is on fire' he was shouting. In a daze, I climbed out of the car. My head hurt, but I wasn't injured besides that."

Val takes a breath and I wait for her to continue.

"Sawyer was right, the car was on fire. All I could think was we had to get to Justin. I ran around the car to his door. It was smashed and unable to open. I started panicking. I ran back to the passenger side and climbed in again. He was still in his seatbelt, but unconscious and covered in blood. With Sawyer's help, I pulled him from the car and onto the grass. There was so much blood," her voice breaks. "That's what brought all this back to me, the blood on you last night." She wipes at her eyes and I find my eyes are wet too.

"You don't have to tell me if you don't want to," I say, reaching for her hand.

She squeezes mine. "I need to tell this. I've kept it bottled up for too many years." She takes another deep breath. "He wasn't breathing so I tried to do CPR. We had learned it in health class, but I never thought I'd need to use it. I'm not even sure I did it right. I pressed his chest as hard as I could, but he'd been cut by a piece of metal and he was so slippery."

Her voice breaks again and I hurt for her.

"I tried to blow into his lungs." She wipes at her mouth. "I can still taste the blood. It didn't work. Sawyer tried to help me. He took over the chest compressions. But each time we pressed his chest, more blood seeped out. The whole time, Justin didn't move, didn't make a sound. The paramedics said he was most likely gone before we pulled him out. This whole time, the car was burning behind us. The heat was horrible and we were afraid the car would explode. So we dragged Justin's body away from the car. I checked for a pulse and couldn't find one. He was gone. I knew he was gone. I threw myself on his body, holding him tight, begging him to stay with me. Sawyer had to pull me off him."

"Oh my, Val. I'm so sorry," I say when she stops. "I can't even imagine."

"After that, I was numb. Every time I closed my eyes, I'd see his mangled, bloodied body. Whenever I licked my lips, I could taste his blood on them. The next months were horrible. I honestly don't know how I got through them, or the years that followed. I never talked to Sawyer again. It was too painful."

The words hang heavy in the air. I have no idea what to say.

"All I wanted was to see Justin again, to talk to him one more time," she says after several moments. "And that's why I called you tonight."

"Me?"

"I've often felt him with me. Like he's watching over me. I

felt him a lot at first, but then it faded. Lately, I keep thinking I see him. I think his spirit is on this property and I want you to find him, to talk to him."

"Aunt Val, he might not be here."

She stands and leans on the porch railing, peering into the trees. "He's here. I can feel him now."

I search the trees, but only see shadows cast by the moon. My back isn't tingling either. "I'm sorry, I don't think he's here."

"Can you try? I know you've called spirits to you before."

"Of course, I can try. But I don't want to disappoint you if I can't find him."

She gives a little laugh. "You can't disappoint me. I know it's a long shot. I just thought, if you called to him, maybe he'd answer."

"And if he does?"

"Tell him I'm sorry."

"You have nothing to be sorry for."

She squeezes the railing. "I do. You see, that car, the one that came over the center line. Well, Justin would have swerved to miss it, except..."

"Val, what happened?"

"Sawyer and I were being stupid. We were playing music really loud and singing along. One of the lines of the song said something about hiding your eyes. So I reached over and covered Justin's eyes."

"Oh no," I whisper.

"That's when the car crossed the line." She wraps her arms around her. "It's my fault he died."

EIGHTEEN

RYLAN FLYNN

"You can't believe that was your fault. It was the other car that went over the line."

"I know what I know. If I hadn't been messing around, he could have missed it. Instead, he paid for my mistake. Now, with your help, maybe I can make some sort of amends."

"You know I'll do what I can, but I don't think he's here."

"But I feel him sometimes. He watches over me." She's practically begging.

"I'll try." I listen to the frogs sing, listen to the sounds beyond. I say a silent prayer that I can help Val. Then I step off the porch, cross the small yard and enter the trees. I shiver when I think of the last time I saw a spirit in these woods.

Val puts George in the cabin and follows me into the dark. "What do we do?" she asks, barely above a whisper.

"I'm not sure." I wish Mickey was with me, I wish Dad was here, although it probably doesn't matter. I seriously doubt the spirit of Justin is here, but I try anyway.

I take both Val's hands in mine. "Now, clear your mind of everything except Justin. Picture him as he was, healthy and happy."

"Okay," she says, her eyes closed.

I'm suddenly very nervous. If Justin is here, he's likely in the same state he was when he died, broken and covered in blood. I steel myself for the possible vision.

"Justin Beckley, Valerie would like to speak to you, to see you one more time," I say into the darkness. I don't get a tingle that he or any ghost might be near. I repeat my plea several times, but nothing happens.

Val's hands begin to sweat. "Let's take a break," I say and let her go.

"He has to be here," Val says. "I just know it."

"I'm sorry."

She looks all around us, as if Justin will walk out of the trees. "Justin, show yourself. I need to talk to you," she calls loudly.

A little sizzle starts at my tail bone. I try not to get too excited. "I feel something."

The wind picks up and lifts my hair. Branches creak overhead mixing with the sounds of the woods.

Val looks at me with eyes bright in the pale moonlight. "He's here, isn't he?"

I grab her hands again and look up into the branches. "Lord, let him come to us. Let him talk to us."

On our right, a shadow grows darker, takes the form of a man. "I see something," I whisper.

Val looks to where I'm staring. "Is it him? I don't see anything."

The form looks like a man, but it is just shadow. The sensations in my back have grown stronger. "Is that you, Justin?" I ask.

The shadow form nods.

"It nodded," I tell Val. "Thank you for coming. Val wants to talk to you."

The form takes a step closer, but is still just a dark shape.

"Justin, I've missed you," Val croaks. "It's been so long."

He takes another step closer, the shadow taking a more solid form.

"Where's Sawyer?" The words barely a breath on the rising wind.

"He said, 'Where's Sawyer?'" I tell her.

"Why would he want Sawyer?"

The shadow grows fainter, losing power. "Bring Sawyer," it says, then disappears.

I tell Val what he said. "Come back," Val pleads. "Forget Sawyer."

The form is gone. My back has no tingles. Even the wind has died down. "He isn't here anymore."

"But he was here," she says triumphantly. "I knew he was here somewhere." She lets go of my hands and claps hers together. "I knew it. He still cares."

She is so excited, I don't have the heart to point out he only wanted to talk to his one-time best friend.

"Now what? How do we bring his spirit back?"

"We can't tonight. He obviously doesn't have much energy or I would have been able to see him clearly. He was just a shadow form. I'm surprised he could even talk to me."

"And he only asked for Sawyer. That's curious." She grows thoughtful. "Wonder why he wants him."

"Do you think we can convince Sawyer to come here and try again?"

"I don't know. Like I said, I haven't talked to him since that night. Even at the funeral, I avoided him."

"That was a long time ago."

"I know. But if he and I hadn't been playing around in the car, singing so loud and all, things would have been different. Justin and I would have been married. We would have a family of our own." She looks to the cabin. "I've never loved anyone since. It was Justin or nothing."

The words make me so sad. Val seems to have a good life, a nice property, a business, a family that loves her. I never wondered if she was lonely. The cabin way back in the woods suddenly seems like an exile, not a refuge.

"It's late," I say. "Let's call it a night." I start toward the cabin. Val hesitates. "You don't want to try again now?"

"He won't be able to come tonight. Let him rest. Maybe with Sawyer here, he'll be stronger."

Val seems unconvinced but follows me anyway. I stop at the bottom of the steps. The moon has climbed a long way across the sky.

"You must be exhausted," Val says, rubbing my upper arm. "Thank you for coming."

The late night last night and the adventures of today have caught up to me. I'm very tired. "I'm so glad we saw him."

"Me, too."

"What are you going to do about Sawyer?"

"I'm not sure. How do I explain all this to him?"

"Want me to talk to him with you?"

"Would you?"

"I'd do anything for you," I tell her. And I would.

NINETEEN

RYLAN FLYNN

I know she might not want to talk to me, but I need Mickey. I want to tell her about going back to the mansion. I want to tell her about Val and Justin. I need to give her the broken camera back.

I keep telling myself not to bother, to give her space. I manage to stay away until afternoon, then I can't take it anymore. We've never had a fight, or a whatever this is. There's barely been a day that I haven't talked to her since her first day in seventh grade, when she moved here from Lafayette.

She walked into science class, clutching her bag to her chest. She had dark curls, a sharp contrast to my limp, straight hair. I was instantly envious. Her eyes were huge and scared. I knew that feeling. She was assigned to the seat next to me. I managed a shy smile of welcome. She smiled back.

At lunch, I invited her to sit with me. She eagerly accepted. I didn't tell her I usually sat alone.

We talked the whole time, like we already knew each other. Until she came, I had been a loner. Alone with the secret I carried and the ghosts I could see.

Eventually, she was the first one I told.

She was the first one that understood me.

Now I sit in front of her house, wondering what went wrong. Not understanding at all.

I watch her house for longer than is polite, wondering if the neighbors see me in my huge tan car. I tell myself to leave, tell myself to go to the door.

I stay in the car, afraid.

Eventually, Marco comes outside, a trash bag in hand. He glances my way, then focuses on the car. I can tell by the tense set of his shoulders that he sees me. And I'm not welcome.

After tossing the bag in the can, he walks to the curb, his face stern. I run the passenger window down and he leans in.

"Rylan, why are you sitting out here?" There's an edge to his voice that I've never heard before. Marco has always been kind to me in the past.

"I—I was hoping to talk to Mickey."

"I thought she told you she needs a break."

"She did, but I don't understand." I feel like I'm back in middle school, scared and friendless.

He leans closer, his eyes intense. "What's not to understand? My wife came home covered in blood. Because she was with you."

I flinch at the harsh words. "That wasn't my fault."

"You took her to that house."

This time, I physically move away from him. I've never seen him so angry.

"Marco, you can't blame me for what happened."

"What you two are doing is dangerous. Look what's happened to you recently."

I can't argue that point, so I don't.

"But Mickey is my best friend," I plead miserably.

"If you are her friend, you'll want her to be safe. You are trouble, Rylan. Chasing ghosts and getting involved in murders, that isn't what Mickey needs."

"Mickey can make her own decisions." I lift my chin a fraction of an inch.

"You think this is about me? This is coming straight from Mickey. She was scared half to death the other night. She should have been home safe and sound, not watching a woman die."

The words hit like a slap. He's right and I have no way to defend myself.

Over his shoulder, I see Mickey step out the front door. She sees Marco talking to me, but doesn't come across the yard. Instead, she crosses her arms over her chest and watches.

The small gesture hurts more than I can imagine.

"I have her camera," I say, handing the broken machine through the window.

Marco grows angrier when he sees the lens hanging loose.

"I didn't break it," I hurry to say.

"But it got broken with you."

That's not fair and tears suddenly sting my eyes. "Tell her I'm sorry," I say and run the window up before Marco can see me cry.

I drive home wiping my eyes and telling myself it will be okay. I have no idea if it will. Mickey and I have never had a situation like this.

Then I see a welcome sight.

Garage sale.

A short time later, I've filled my back seat with items I can't live without. A selection of carnival glass that glittered so prettily in the sun I couldn't pass it up. Two throw pillows with funny sayings embroidered on them. The pillows made me smile, so I added them to my pile. A clock that looks old, but runs on batteries. A wooden box that I just couldn't say no to.

The final treasure I find is a salt-and-pepper shaker set in the shape of chickens. They are painted in bright colors and, for the moment, they make the pain go away.

When I get home, I take the items inside and add them to the piles in the packed front room. In my mind, I had places picked out for each item. Now, the reality of my stuffed house weighs on me.

I end up throwing the box onto a stack, not caring if it gets broken. The pillows, I toss toward where the couch is buried. The carnival glass, I shove onto an already overcrowded shelf. I have no place for the clock, so I sit it on a random pile.

The chicken salt-and-pepper shakers I take into my room. I set them on the overflowing night table. The chickens seem to be smiling. I focus on the smiles, pull Darby close to my chest and sit on the bed, the only place to sit in the house. His fur smells like baby powder with a hint of mustiness. I breathe it in, his fluff tickling my nose.

"She'll get over it," I tell Darby. "We've been through worse."

The words are hollow. We haven't been through anything like this before. Mickey has been the one person I could count on through everything.

My heart hurts, my head hurts. I want to go to sleep.

"Rylan, are you hungry?" Mom calls from her room.

I jump up eagerly.

I may not have any friends left. But at least I have my mom, even if she is dead.

TWENTY

RYLAN FLYNN

At Mom's suggestion, I make a sandwich. Most of my plates are dirty, so I eat it over the sink. When I'm done, I stare out the window, not sure what to do next. Normally, Mickey and I would be working on the show or making plans for another episode or even just hanging out. It breaks my heart to know that might all be in the past.

I'm startled by the sudden thought. If *Beyond the Dead* ends, and it might, what will I do for money? How long can the show bring in revenue if we don't make new episodes? Mickey handles all the promotional stuff, so now what do I do without her? Losing her as a friend is bad enough. Losing the show as well is just too much.

At least my bills are low. The house and the car are both paid off thanks to Mom. I have a little savings. How long can that last?

So many questions swirl in my head I feel dizzy.

In addition to my own personal concerns, there's the very real threat of a killer in town. And then there's the situation with Aunt Val, Justin and Sawyer.

I'll focus on what I can control.

I call Aunt Val. First, to ask if I can pick up a few shifts at The Hole just in case. Second, to make plans for talking to Sawyer.

"Of course you can do a few shifts," Val says when I ask. "Eileen will be happy for the help. Does this have to do with you and Mickey's situation?"

"Mostly. A little extra cash never hurts, especially if the show is on break for a while."

"You really think this break will last?"

I tell her about my run-in with Marco this morning.

"That doesn't sound good," she says.

"It really wasn't." I run a finger across the edge of the kitchen counter. "She just stood there and watched me."

"She's scared, Ry. What you guys went through was awful. Give her time and she'll move past it." She doesn't sound very convincing.

"You think?"

"You two have been friends for so long it will take more than this to end your relationship. Just give her space."

"I can do that. Now speaking of friends, what are we going to do about Justin and Sawyer? Do you still want to go forward? We don't have to."

She takes so long to answer I'm afraid I've upset her. "I want to. But I don't know how to approach him. I can't just show up on his front step and say 'do you want to help me contact a ghost?'"

"Actually, that's what we should do. I'll go with you and do the talking."

Val sighs. "Are you serious?"

"Why not? I know him from my Declan days. I think he knows what I do. The worst that can happen is he says no."

"He might just do that. Then what?"

"We'll cross that bridge if it happens." I check the clock. "How about in an hour? I'll meet you at his house."

"What if he's not home?"

"What if he is?"

"That's what I'm afraid of."

Not much has changed at Sawyer's house since the time Declan brought me here for dinner. The bushes out front are a little higher, maybe. It only adds to the imposing nature of the place. A sprawling ranch in one of Ashby's nicer neighborhoods, the house seems like a lot for a bachelor. Then again, Sawyer and his sister, Declan's mom, come from money.

Val isn't here yet, so I sit in my car on the street in front of his house. I listen to music and practice what I should say to Sawyer.

While I think, I chew on a thumb nail. Then I see my little finger still has a spot of blood in the cuticle. I pull my hand away from my face. How had that spot made it through two showers and several hand washings?

I rub at the stain, but it won't budge. I find a half-drunk bottle of water on the floor board and stick my finger in. I soak the finger, wiggling it a little. When I take the finger out I rub hard until the blood is finally gone.

I check my other fingers closely to be sure they are all clean.

I'm so intent on studying my hands that I'm startled when Val knocks on my driver's side window. I jump and drop the bottle of water on my lap. The cold water seeps between my legs and I feel it spreading up the back of my jeans.

"Holy flip," I exclaim, trying to get away from the water, but failing.

I open the door and dart from the wet seat, wiping at my rear.

"What happened?" Val says, confused at the little dance I'm doing on the street.

"You scared me and I spilled water all over myself." Looking down, I see the damage. I definitely look like I wet my pants.

Val can't help but laugh a little. "I'm sorry. I waved several times, but you didn't look up."

I look at the dark stain on my jeans, wondering if I should go home and change before we talk to Sawyer. I'm about to ask Val if she'll wait for me, when a car slows down behind me. The car stops and rolls its window down.

"Rylan Flynn? What are you doing here?" Sawyer Lambert says with pleasure. His eyes dart to my wet pants and back to my face.

Too late to change now.

"I came to talk to you." I lean toward the car window. "Me and my Aunt Val."

Sawyer looks to Val then does a double take.

"Valerie Flynn," he says breathlessly. "Well, this is a surprise."

"Can we talk?" I ask.

"Yes, yes. Come up to the house. I'm just getting home from work," he says in a rush. Obviously, seeing Val has thrown him.

He drives up the long driveway to the oversized garage. Val and I walk up the drive behind the car.

"Ready for this?" I ask.

"No. But I have to do it, for Justin."

I give her hand a quick squeeze. "We've got this."

Sawyer meets us at the front sidewalk. His eyes slide to the stain on my pants again, a question in his eyes.

"It's nothing. I spilled water," I tell him.

"Of course." He dares to look at Val. "Good to see you, Valerie," he says with obvious affection. If I didn't know better I'd say there was chemistry in the air. When I look at Val, her cheeks are a little pinker than usual.

"Good to see you, Sawyer." Her voice is soft.

We stand on the sidewalk for a long moment. "Oh, come inside," he says. "It's getting warm out here."

It's not really warm, but we follow him up the walk to the wide concrete covered porch. At one end is a hanging swing and a matching chair.

"Can we sit out here?" Val says.

"Sure. I don't use the porch enough. It will be a nice change." He takes a seat in the chair and Val and I settle on the blue floral swing cushions. My toes barely touch the floor and I feel like a child sitting with the adults. I stand back up and lean against the rail instead.

Val's feet touch just fine and she pushes herself back and forth in a slow rhythm.

Sawyer looks from me to her and says, "So, you mentioned you wanted to talk to me? Is this about what happened at Declan's? He was pretty shook up when he got here."

"It's not about that," I say then pause to see if Val will take over. She doesn't, so I dive in. "Back when Declan and I were dating, did he ever mention to you what I do for a living?"

Sawyer blinks in surprise. "If you mean the show where you talk to ghosts, then yes. I've actually seen a few episodes."

Now I'm surprised, and flattered. "Really?"

"I was curious. The show is fascinating."

"I really appreciate that."

"Is that why you came here? Is this about your show?"

"Not exactly. But it is about a ghost," I say, looking again at Val to see if she wants to talk.

"It's about Justin," she says flatly.

Sawyer sits back in his chair, his shoulders slumping. "I was afraid you'd say something like that when I saw you came with Rylan. What about him?"

"We saw him," Val says, excited. "Well, Rylan saw him."

"That's not possible," he says.

I step away from the railing. "It is and it happened. Last night."

Sawyer stands and paces the porch, runs a hand through his short brown hair. "If anyone else told me this, I'd say they were crazy. But you, I mean, is this real? Justin is a ghost?"

"It's real. He isn't very strong, mostly just a shape. But he was there in the woods. He asked for you."

His eyes widen in surprise. "Me? What could he want with me?"

"That's what we want to find out," Val says. "He said 'bring Sawyer.' If that's what he wants that's what I'll do."

"I see," he says, halting his pacing. "You want me to talk to him with you?" He places both hands on the back of the chair and locks eyes with Val. Something unnamable passes between them. "I'll do it."

TWENTY-ONE

Gone. She is gone.

My most recent plaything has left.

I wasn't done with her, had more fun planned. Now all my plans are dashed. I'm torn between relief it is over and a soul-deep itch for another.

The blades I used on her are still on the work bench. I gather them up and open the cabinet of tools. The little farmer figurine smiles out at me, his straw hat eternally crooked.

"You need another," the figurine says.

"I don't want another," I lie. It feels like the right thing to say, the correct answer.

"You need another," it repeats.

I shove my hands against my ears to block the voice. It does no good. "You know who you truly are and you need to play."

I hang my head. "I will. I know just the one."

"This time don't let her get away," the cursed figurine says. I take something from the cabinet and shut the door tight.

"She won't get away," I reply.

TWENTY-TWO

MARCO RAMIREZ

My back aches from mopping floors at the middle school all evening. I stretch in the seat as I drive home, trying to release the tension. It doesn't work. I'm keyed up from more than work.

I'm upset by Mickey and Rylan. I love Rylan, but she gets Mickey into all kinds of trouble.

I'll do whatever I need to do to keep Mickey safe.

I turn the corner leading to home, and I think of Mickey home tonight. No more late-night romps into abandoned buildings chasing dead people. No more crime scenes. No more murders.

Mickey is home safe, waiting for me.

The front porch light is not on when I pull into the driveway. Mickey always leaves it on for me, even if she's out for the night. I don't think on it too much and park in the garage.

I gather my lunch cooler from the front seat of the car and enter the kitchen. The kitchen light isn't on either, another thing Mickey normally does. I reach for the switch and put my cooler on the counter.

With the light on, I can see into the dining room. Two

chairs are lying on their sides. Curious, I cross the kitchen, calling out to Mickey.

She doesn't answer.

I pick one of the chairs up and flip the switch for the front room.

My blood runs cold when I see the mess there. The coffee table is smashed and the cushions are half off the couch. A vase that normally sits on the book shelf is shattered, the glass pieces strewn across the floor.

"Mickey!" I scream, running down the hall to the bedrooms and her office. I check each room, but I can't find her. I double back and check the closets and even under the beds. Her office has been ransacked, the computers and monitors thrown on the floor.

I spin in the room, confused and terrified.

Where is my wife?

My lungs hurt and I realize I'm panting. I take a steadying breath and hurry back to my lunch cooler in the kitchen to find my phone.

When the 911 operator answers, I yell, "I think my wife has been kidnapped."

TWENTY-THREE

RYLAN FLYNN

I've never driven so fast through town. I don't care if I get pulled over. The Ashby Police have more to worry about tonight than my driving. I needn't have worried. There are so many cars at Mickey's house I doubt anyone is on traffic patrol.

The yellow tape is already up. Officer Frazier guards the perimeter and sees me running down the block toward the tape. He makes like he's going to stop me, but I just give him a stern look and duck under the tape.

"You know you can't be here," he says in his best cop voice.

"I can and I will. Just try to stop me." He takes a step toward me and I ready myself to fight my way in. "It's Mickey," I say miserably. "I can't stay away."

"It's not protocol." He takes another step closer, reaching for my arm.

"Take it up with Ford," I say, brushing his hand away and darting across the yard full of uniforms. I search through the dark blue shirts for Marco and find him sitting on a porch chair talking to Tyler. I hurry to his side.

"I'm here," I say, putting my hand on his shoulder. Whatever drama went on this morning, I care deeply for him and hate to see him hurting.

Marco looks up in surprise and then his shoulders slump.

Tyler, for his part, doesn't seem too surprised to see me. "Do you know anything at all? Did she say she was going somewhere? Or had a new friend? Any hint of who might have taken her?" he asks.

"I don't know a thing," I tell him. "You're sure she was taken? She didn't just go out to the store or for a walk?"

Marco hangs his head.

"There's sign of a struggle in the house. From the looks of it, Mickey put up one hell of a fight," Ford says behind me.

I spin to face him. I see Officer Frazier coming through the throng of officers out front. "Is it okay I'm here? Frazier's coming to throw me out."

Ford holds a hand up to Frazier, indicating I can stay. He backs away, but doesn't look happy about it.

"You're sure Mickey fought?" I stand on tiptoe trying to see into the house.

"You can't go in there," Ford says. "The crime scene techs are working the scene right now. If I let you stay, you have to promise not to go in."

"I promise," I say reluctantly.

"It's a mess," Marco says. "Chairs knocked over, the coffee table broken. In her office, they trashed her computers and monitors and video equipment." He turns a tortured face up to us. "Who would do this?"

"Don't worry, we'll find her," I say, although inside I'm terrified. "What do we know?" I ask Ford and Tyler.

"Not much. There are no lights on, so we think she was taken before sunset, but that gives us a pretty big window. We're canvassing the neighbors right now, but nothing has come from it yet."

"Be sure to talk to Mrs. Tamaka. She's constantly watching

the neighborhood." Marco points across the street to a house two doors down. "She likes to sit on her porch and watch everyone. She's honestly kind of a pain, but maybe her nosy ways will help out for once."

Ford and Tyler look at the house in question. The front light is on and we can see an officer on her porch. "Looks like they're talking to her now," Tyler says.

Since I don't know what else to do, I take a seat next to Marco. "Now what?" I ask Ford.

He seems bothered by the question. "First we wait for the canvas to be completed and hope for something from that. At the same time, we wait for the CSI techs to finish up. Hopefully they'll find something, prints or DNA or anything that will lead us to a suspect." As I listen to Ford, a shadow flickers behind him. Before I can get a good look it's gone.

"So we wait?" Marco asks miserably. "That's it?"

"That's what you do," Ford says. "We have a long way to go and need a direction to go in."

"But Mickey could be hurt or—"

"I'm sure Mickey is not hurt. I'm sure we'll find her safe and sound," I reassure him, but the words sound hollow, even to me. I see the shadow flicker again and realize my back is tingling with more than fear. It's the little boy I've sensed here before.

"We don't have any witnesses," Ford says. "At least, not that we know of yet."

"We might have a witness," I venture.

Ford's mouth grows tight. "What do you mean?" I can tell by his tone he has an idea of what I'm about to say.

"There might be an otherworld witness," I say.

Ford and Tyler brighten at the idea.

Marco looks confused.

"I'm sorry, Marco. But your house is haunted."

He stares at me a long moment. "Rylan, I'm not in the mood for this tonight," he says, slightly angry.

"Just hear me out. Several times, I've sensed the spirit of a small boy here. I've never really seen him, he's more like a feeling, an energy."

"But you know it's a young boy?" Ford asks.

"I don't know for sure, but that's the sense I get. And he's here tonight. I just saw a flicker of shadow behind you. I'm pretty sure it's him."

"And he might have seen what happened to Mickey," Ford finishes for me, warming to the idea.

"Exactly."

"This is nuts. My house is not haunted," Marco says.

"Most places are, just no one knows it. If he can help find Mickey, isn't it worth trying to talk to him?" I ask.

Marco's face is a mix of disgust and hope.

"Do what you can," he finally says. "Anything to save Mickey."

TWENTY-FOUR

RYLAN FLYNN

"Wait a minute," Tyler says, holding a hand up. "Rylan, you know I support what you do, but this is currently a crime scene. We can't just start looking for ghosts in the middle of it."

"But—"

"He's right," Ford says with obvious disappointment. "This isn't like the other times when the scene was closed."

"But if we wait, who knows what might happen." My voice cracks.

"It's pushing it to even let you this far," Ford says. "I can only do so much."

"What is my sister trying to convince you of now?" Keaton joins us on the porch dressed in a suit.

"Keaton, glad you made it," Ford says, shaking his hand.

Keaton takes his hand, but his eyes are on me. "Why are you here?" he asks, not unkindly.

"It's Mickey. Of course I'm here."

"I mean on this side of the tape. You could compromise the scene. We don't want to give any reason to a defense attorney to discredit what we find here."

I hate that he's talking like a lawyer. Hate even more that he's right.

I stand, feeling horrible but unable to leave. "We were just discussing the little boy ghost that haunts this house. Maybe I can talk to him and get some idea of what happened."

Keaton almost laughs out loud. "Now that would definitely be fodder for a defense attorney. A séance at the scene. You know you can't do that."

"It's not a séance and it might help."

"It might be the thing that gets the kidnapper off."

"But we have to catch him first." I step closer to my brother, my blood singing in my veins in anger.

"We will catch him. Our way. You can't help in this." He doesn't back down, uses all of the five inches of height he has on me to be imposing. It's a trick he's used since we were kids. He's never put a hand on me, not even in our worst fights back in the day. He only had to stand tall and I would back down.

I resist the urge to raise on my tiptoes to look him directly in the eye.

Ford intervenes as he always did. He puts a hand between us. "Okay, okay. We all want the same thing here."

"Look, Rylan. I'm really sorry that Mickey is missing. You know I love her too. But we have to do this by the book and be careful that we get this guy."

"Do I have a say?" Marco, who had been quietly watching, chimes in.

"Not really," Keaton says. "This is a law matter now."

"But if Rylan has a way to help find Mickey, I want to use it," Marco says.

I'm relieved Marco still believes in me, but Keaton blows air in exasperation. He looks to Tyler for help. Tyler only shrugs, staying out of it.

"You know I can't let you in the house," Ford says to me. "What if she does it in the side yard?" he asks Keaton.

He rolls his eyes. "You guys just won't let this go. What if she doesn't even make contact with this spirit and the word gets out you tried this? It would be a disaster."

"I'd rather save Mickey and deal with a disaster than just sit here when we could be helping," I say, sensing a crack in him. "That's all that matters right now. Finding Mickey."

Keaton rubs his face in frustration. "In the side yard?" he says.

"Right. I can go by myself. No one needs to know."

Keaton exchanges a long look with Ford. In the end it's really his decision as head detective.

"We all have the same goal here," I push. "It should only take a few moments. No one needs to know."

"And if you do get some good information, where do we say it came from?" Keaton says, always planning his case.

I smile, knowing I've won. "An anonymous tip."

He shakes his head and raises his hands in surrender. "I've done what I can. It's up to you, Ford."

Ford looks torn, but gives me a tight-lipped nod.

"Thank you," Marco says to the group.

"Make it quick," Ford adds as I slink around the garage.

The darkness of the side yard engulfs me and nerves flutter in my belly. I talked so big about being able to help, I really need to deliver. Truth is, my back is not tingling and I've only seen glimpses of shadows to let me know the spirit is here. I'm not even sure it is a little boy. I just get that energy from it.

How in the world am I supposed to talk to him from out in the yard? Keaton is not wrong. If word gets out that I'm even trying to contact the ghost it could hurt the case. What if I do this and don't get anything and mess things up after all?

Dad would tell me to focus on the task and worry about the rest later.

He'd also tell me to pray.

I find a place near the back wall of the house, but out of the light pouring through the windows. I drop to my knees and bow my head, my hands clasped in front of me.

"Lord, please, please help me talk to this spirit and find Mickey. Please put a hedge of protection around her, wherever she is. Let this boy know something that will lead us to her." I don't know what else to say, so I add an amen and open my eyes.

The sounds of activity from inside the house reach the dark yard. I try to block it out. I focus on my back, willing it to tingle. I get the lightest touch of something. Maybe it's wishful thinking.

I listen to the breeze in the branches of the large oak tree in the middle of the neighbor's yard. I look up to the stars overhead. The moon hides behind a cloud, making it glow. It's lovely. In another time and place, I'd take a moment and admire the vision in the sky.

Now, I just focus on the universe, on the energy, on the beyond. I reach my hands to the sky, open palmed, hoping to make contact. My fingers block some of the stars. I focus on the spaces between them, on the pinpricks of light.

My pocket vibrates and, at first, I think it is a sign from beyond. When the sound of Val's ring-tone screeches across the yard, I realize it's my phone.

I fumble in my pocket to quiet the phone. My hands are shaking so hard I can barely answer the call.

"Hello?" I gasp.

"Rylan are you okay?"

"Not really. Mickey's been kidnapped. Val, I've gotta go." I hang up the phone.

The little boy ghost stands before me, clear as day.

TWENTY-FIVE

RYLAN FLYNN

The ghost of the boy stares at me with obvious interest. He looks to be about seven or eight. His hair is matted with blood on one side and his face is torn and bloodied. His left arm hangs at an odd angle, broken below the shoulder. Whatever happened to his body in death wasn't pretty.

I manage not to flinch at the sight and say, "Hello."

He seems startled that I can see him and want to talk to him. He flickers away for a moment then comes back.

"You can see me?" he asks, his voice sweet and full of hope.

"I see you. Will you talk to me?"

He disappears again and I worry he won't come back this time. A long moment later, he returns.

"I'll talk," he says.

"Did you see what happened here earlier?"

"Police."

"Right the police are here. Before that, when Mickey was home? Did you see who took her?"

He flickers again like a bad TV picture. I wait until he grows strong enough to talk again.

"Bad things happened."

"Yes. Bad things. Do you know who hurt her?"

"Miss Mickey fought him."

"It was a him, a man?"

"I think so."

"Did you know the man?"

"No." He steps away from me, agitated. "Bad man. Very bad."

"What did he look like?" I push.

"A very dark man. He hurt Miss Mickey." He starts to cry and fades to a shadow shape.

"Please don't go," I step toward the shadow and it disintegrates into nothing.

I wait for him to gather energy to return.

I wait a long time, but he doesn't reappear. Not even a shadow or a flicker or a tingle in my back. He's gone.

Not wanting to leave, just in case, I lean against the house and scan the yard for any sign of the little boy. An owl hoots nearby, making me jump.

After a while, I know it's futile to keep waiting. I've learned all I can from the spirit. I go back around the garage to the front of the house. Marco is still sitting on the porch, but Ford, Keaton and Tyler must have gone inside.

Marco looks up with hope in his eyes when I approach. "Did you talk to it?"

"I did. He was scared and didn't say much except a bad man took Mickey."

"That's it?" he's disappointed. "We already knew a bad person took her."

"Now we know it's a man," I offer, knowing it isn't much.

"So that narrows it down to half the population, great." He sinks his head into his hands.

"It's something."

Marco looks despondent. "Look, I know I called you, but maybe you should leave."

The words sting. "I want to help."

"You've done all you can," he says. "Leave this to the police."

Through the front door, I catch Keaton watching me. He doesn't look any more inviting than Marco sounds. I peer in, but don't see Ford. An officer comes out the door and I have to step out of the way.

Maybe Marco is right. I'm in the way here.

"Tell Ford and Tyler what the ghost said about a dark man."

"You only said a bad man before. Now you said dark. As in skin color?"

"I don't think so. I think he meant dark like bad energy."

"That's not much help either."

I'm growing impatient with this attitude but hold my tongue. "Guess not, but tell Ford anyway."

"I will." Marco looks away.

I start through the throng of officers in the yard toward my car. Officer Frazier holds the tape up for me with the tiniest of smirks.

After all the excitement of the crime scene, my car feels empty and too quiet. "Mickey, where are you?" I say, looking at the house across the street from where I'm parked. It's the house Marco said the overly curious neighbor lives in. Mrs. Tamaka.

The porch light is still on and Mrs. Tamaka is there watching the activity down the block. Her poof of white hair is bright under the porch light.

On impulse, I open the car door. She's so focused on the police presence she doesn't notice me until I'm at the bottom of her porch steps.

"Mrs. Tamaka?" I ask, my hand on the rail.

She turns quickly, startled.

"Yes. Can I help you?" she asks in a tightly polite tone.

"I know they already talked to you, but I wonder if I could ask you a few questions as well."

"Are you with the police?" Her eyes slide over my t-shirt, skinny jeans and black sneakers. "You don't look like an officer."

"I'm not with the police, at least not officially." I go up the steps and offer her my hand. "I'm Rylan Flynn."

She had been reaching for my hand, but drops hers suddenly. "Now that you're in the light, I recognize you. You're that ghost girl that's always coming to the Ramirez house. You have that show on the computer."

I drop my hand that she won't touch. "That's right. I'm Mickey Ramirez's best friend."

"Such a shame what happened there."

"As you can imagine, we are all really shook up and want to bring Mickey back home safe."

"As I told the officer, I don't know what happened to her. I didn't see anything."

Something flickers in her eyes and I get the feeling she's hiding information. Maybe it's wishful thinking.

"Anything at all might help find her. I understand you keep a pretty good eye on the neighborhood, maybe you saw someone lurking around. A strange car or a man you didn't recognize."

"I didn't see a thing." She lifts her chin and smooths her poof of hair. "I'm not a snoop. I just keep an eye on my neighbors to keep them safe."

"Then this is the perfect opportunity to help." I'm beginning to sound desperate. "You must have seen something today, or maybe in the previous days. Anything suspicious."

"Young lady, if I could help, I would. I've been gone most of the day. My daughter took me to a doctor's appointment then I went to her house for dinner. Then I went to bed."

She looks me straight in the eyes and I know she's telling the truth. I feel deflated.

"I'm sorry, I thought maybe—"

"I know, dear. It's okay. I truly hope they find your friend safe and sound."

"We will," I say with more conviction than I actually feel. "We have to."

At a loss for what else I can do, I retreat down the steps and back to my car. I don't want to leave, but there is nothing more I can accomplish. Mickey is probably miles away from here by now.

Unless...

I turn on the sidewalk and look at Mrs. Tamaka's house. There is a light on in the front room, but the rest of the house is dark. Could Mickey be here?

Mrs. Tamaka watches me from the porch. A little old lady is a far cry from a bad man full of darkness. I need to think clearly to find Mickey, not grasp at wild straws.

With no other options, I drive around the neighborhood street by street. I search the alleys, not at all sure what I'm hoping to find. Mickey walking down the sidewalk toward home?

I broaden my search and drive for a long time. Ashby isn't too large and it only takes an hour or two until I've driven down every road in town.

No Mickey.

Just as I feared.

I work my way back to my own house and pull into my driveway. I sit with the headlights shining on my garage door.

Then the dam breaks and all the fear I'd managed to keep under control pours out.

I lean my head against my steering wheel and cry until my chest hurts.

She has to be okay. She just has to.

My nose is running so I dig through the glove box for the stash of drive-thru napkins I keep there.

A hair tie that belongs to Mickey is among the napkins. The sight of it makes me begin to cry all over. I take it out and slide it on my wrist with a snap. The tiny pain is comforting somehow.

I focus on the little sting and not on the massive ache in my heart. Images of Mickey flash through my mind, each one breaking me just a little more.

I have to find her, but I have no idea where to even start. She could be anywhere in Ashby or beyond.

"Mickey!" I scream into the car, beating on the steering wheel.

A second set of headlights on the garage door joins mine. I wipe my eyes with the damp napkin and look to the car. I half-expect it to be Dad checking on me.

It's a police cruiser.

I'd recognize the silhouette in the driver's seat anywhere.

Ford has come.

TWENTY-SIX

RYLAN FLYNN

He leaves his headlights on and I leave mine, four shafts of light in the late-night darkness of my neighborhood. I scramble out of the car as he climbs out of his and rounds into the lights.

I don't think.

I go to him.

He catches me in his arms as I collapse against his chest.

"It's okay," he says into my hair.

"No, it's not." Pressing my forehead to the open collar of his polo, I can feel his chest hair below my skin. My face is hot from crying and his cool chest feels lovely.

"We'll find her. I promise you." He runs a hand down my back.

"Don't make promises you can't keep," I say miserably, wrapping my arms around his chest. His belt with its many tools presses into my belly.

He takes my face in his hands and looks directly in my eyes. "We will find her."

I melt at his confidence. The world disappears and all that matters is his blue eyes, then his lips so close.

"Rylan?" I can feel his breath on my lips, warm and sweet.

"Yes?" I lean a fraction of an inch closer, barely daring to believe this is happening. The world disappears. I feel the heat of his body against mine, the warmth of his hands in my hair.

In the distance, a car backfires with a loud *bang*.

We both jump and his hand goes to his hip in reflex. His other hand presses me closer to his chest.

I laugh nervously. "That scared me."

The spell is broken and we release each other. I feel a deep sense of loss, but cover it with another nervous laugh. "I didn't know cars even did that anymore."

"Old ones do."

My hair feels hot and heavy down my back and I pull it into a ponytail. Cool night air blows against my hot neck. I quickly realize the tie on my wrist is Mickey's.

I drop my hair and return to the present horrible situation.

"Have you found anything out at the crime scene?" I ask, pretending our almost kiss didn't happen.

"Nothing new. No prints. Most likely no DNA, although the techs took samples from just about everything."

"How's Marco holding up?"

"He went to stay with his mom."

"That's good," I say absently. "I wish I had found out more from the little boy. He was pretty shook up. He only said it was a bad man. A dark man."

"Marco told me. I suppose it was too much to hope for, that the ghost would know who took her."

A long moment stretches, the only sound the running engines of our cars.

"Why did you come?" I finally ask.

"To check on you," he says gently. "This can't be easy."

"I'm fine," I lie.

"Ry." He reaches to wipe the remnants of my earlier tears.

"Okay, I'm not fine. But I'm better than Mickey." I hug myself against the late-night chill. He takes me in his arms again, but this time it is more like the friend of my big brother, not the hot energy of before. I accept the comfort he offers and let him wrap me in his arms.

"We will find her," he says again.

I take a deep breath of his cologne, then push away and lean against the hood of his car. "How are we going to do that? What's the next step?"

"Your next step is to get some sleep. It's really late and there's nothing you can do tonight."

"I don't think I can sleep with her gone." Despite my words, I'm bone tired. Talking to the little boy took a lot out of me. He was so weak I had to really work to see him.

"There's nothing you can do. Nothing that even we can do. The canvas didn't give us anything. The scene doesn't give us anything. It's like she was taken out the door and disappeared."

"But she's out there."

"Get some rest, Rylan. Hit it hard in the morning."

"I feel like I need to look for her. I've already been up and down all the streets here in Ashby."

He seems impressed. "Is that why you're still in your car?"

"Yeah. I'm not sure what I was looking for exactly."

"But it's something. It helps."

A sudden yawn catches me by surprise and I cover my mouth.

"Like I said, it's really late. Go to bed, Ry. We'll start again in the morning."

"Do you think Mickey is asleep somewhere?"

He flinches at the question. "Honestly, I hope so."

"He's had her for hours."

"I know. There's nothing else to do tonight. Tomorrow is another day." He pulls me close again for a quick hug that doesn't last near long enough. "I'll see you tomorrow."

With those parting words, he releases me and gets back into his cruiser.

I stand in the driveway, watching him drive away, then I turn my car off.

The front door is still blocked so I have to let myself in through the patio door.

For a crazy moment, I think Mickey will be in the house. But she hasn't been in here since I moved back, and she's not here now.

Instead of Mickey, Mom calls hello from her room.

I drag my tired body down the path to the hall and her door. Mom is sitting on the bed as usual.

"Hello, darling," she says, her brush in her hand. Despite the hole in her head, the sight is a welcome one.

I hurry to the bed and drop to my knees beside it. "Hey, Mom."

"Rough night? You look horrible."

I catch my reflection in her dressing table mirror. My mascara has run and I have dark circles under my eyes. I wipe at them, but they don't go away.

"It's not been a good night," I tell her. "Mickey has been kidnapped."

"Oh no! How awful." From her tone, I don't think she truly understands. Mom has a fragile grasp on reality. "Do you want a sandwich?"

It's almost comical how she asks if I'm hungry after what I just told her. Ghost Mom seems to have a one-track mind, and that track is feeding me.

I curl up on her bed, close to her, but not touching. "I'm not hungry." It's a lie. I'm famished.

"Of course, dear," she says then goes back to brushing her hair. I listen to the brush slide across the strands and the sound soothes me.

"I'm sure she's fine," Mom says after a long moment. "If not, you'll find her."

It's the last thing I hear as I fall asleep curled next to her.

TWENTY-SEVEN

VALERIE FLYNN

I wish I was alone to deal with the news that Mickey has been taken, but Sawyer is sitting on my porch, in the rocker where Rylan normally sits. He arrived a while ago, a few minutes before our agreed-on time.

A little early, just like the Sawyer I remember. Always reliable.

"Everything okay?" he asks, his face full of concern.

I sink into my chair and put a hand on George's head to steady me. "Mickey Ramirez is missing."

He raises his eyebrows in question.

"She's Rylan's best friend. She's pretty shaken up."

"I bet," Sawyer says. "I'm so sorry. Is there anything we can do?"

I notice the *we* and am thankful he's included himself, even though he doesn't know Mickey.

"I don't think so. I guess we wait for news. I'm sure the police are doing all they can. And Rylan will let me know if there's a way to help." I sit on the edge of my chair, worry and fear for Mickey shooting through me. I don't know what to do, or how to act. I haven't seen Sawyer for years, and now this.

"Do you want me to stay?" he asks helpfully, as I remember he always is.

I turn to look at him, not sure how to answer. "I don't know. To tell you the truth, I'm at a loss with all this. I don't even understand why you needed to be here to talk to Justin. Now this with Mickey. It's a little much."

"I'm sure they'll find her," he says gently. "And as for Justin, he's waited years to talk to us, I'm sure he can wait a while longer."

"I suppose so." I try not to sound disappointed. Up until a few minutes ago talking to Justin was all I could think about. Now I'm filled with worry about Mickey.

"Look," Sawyer says, standing. "I think I'll go. We can pick this up when your friend is home safe."

I stand, too. "Thank you. I don't think I can be very good company right now."

"I totally understand. Well, actually I don't, but I do," he says, stumbling on his words. "I guess I'm not good in a crisis."

"You're fine."

He is silent a long moment, then says, "I wasn't back when it mattered." His eyes search mine. It is the first real mention of that terrible night we have made.

"Neither of us were very good that night." I swallow, then continue. "I wonder if I did all I could to save him," I say out loud the thought that has swirled in my head for all these years.

"I wonder the same about myself. I froze and wasn't much help. I've regretted it ever since."

"I don't remember it that way. I only remember the terror." George pushes against my legs, giving me the strength to say the next part. "And the guilt."

"You don't have anything to feel guilty about." He sounds genuine.

"But I was messing around. I covered his eyes."

He takes my hand. "The driver that hit us is to blame. The

rest doesn't matter." His eyes hold mine and I notice a gold fleck in one of the irises. I focus on that fleck.

"Do you really think so?"

"I know so. I was there. We had no chance."

I drop my eyes, unable to keep up the connection. "I have blamed myself all this time," I say just above a whisper.

"Maybe that's what Justin wants for us. He wants us to know it wasn't our fault. I mean, I was fooling around and singing like an idiot too."

I've never thought about Sawyer's role, if any. I'd been too consumed by my own guilt.

"You really think that's what Justin wants now?"

"It could be."

"I wish we could talk to him without Rylan. She's obviously going to be busy and I don't want to bother her."

"We could try," he says.

"I don't think it works like that."

"Some people see ghosts even when they don't have Rylan's gifts." He sounds like he believes what he's saying.

"I don't think I do."

"There's a reason you asked her to contact him in the first place. You had to have had some feeling."

I chew my lower lip in thought. "I did have the sensation he was watching over me. That's a far cry from being able to talk to him."

He shrugs. "Just a thought. Maybe not tonight. But I'm game if you are."

I lean against the porch railing and look up at the moon and stars. A soft breeze is blowing through the trees and the bugs and frogs are singing, the timeless song of the woods. It's almost magical, and I wonder if he's right. Can we contact him?

"He was very weak when he came before. I don't think he's normally here."

"Don't spirits usually stay close to where they died?"

"Usually. But one thing I've learned from Rylan is that spirits don't follow rules."

"What if we went to the site of the accident?"

The words hang heavy on the porch.

"I avoid that place as much as possible," I eventually reply. "I drive out of my way to not pass it."

"Me too, but if Justin is on this side that would be the best place to find him."

I search his face, but only see honesty there. "You think we could?"

"I don't see why we can't try," he says.

"I'm shocked you're so calm about all this. It's not every day someone gets approached about talking to a ghost."

"Honestly, I'm glad this is happening. I've lived with the grief and guilt for too long. If this brings some kind of resolution, then I'm all for it. Honestly, I've kind of wondered if he was around too."

I tighten my grip on the porch railing, my thoughts swirling. "When do you want to do this?" I ask.

"Well, we're up late already. No time like the present."

I hesitate only a moment. "Let's do it."

After putting George in the house, we walk to the driveway and my SUV. "I can drive."

When we are seated and buckled, it hits me what we are about to do. "We're really doing this?"

He rubs his chin nervously. "I guess so." He doesn't sound as confident as he did a few minutes ago. Before I can chicken out, I start the engine and pull down my long lane.

We ride in silence all the way to the site of the crash. I can barely believe Sawyer Lambert is in my vehicle after all these years, and keep darting little looks his way. He has his eyes locked on the passing fields and tree lines.

I pull way over on the shoulder and park the SUV. There is no traffic this late at night. My headlights cut bright swaths into the dark, illuminating a small white cross someone put up on the spot.

"I didn't know that was there," I say, my eyes fixed on the cross with Justin's name on it.

"I didn't either. His family must have put it up."

Goosebumps run down my arms at the sight. I turn off the engine and my lights. I don't want to see the cross.

The dark fills the cab and we sit a few moments in silence, neither of us brave enough to get out.

"Are we really doing this?" I ask again. The whole situation feels surreal, like a bad dream. A dream that I started.

"We don't have to. We can go back." There's a tiny quiver to his voice and I'm glad he's as nervous as I am.

I chew my lower lip, thinking, then let it go. "We're here now. Let's try." Before fear makes me turn back, I climb out onto the roadside. Our closing doors echo across dark corn fields that stretch out from both sides of the road. Not a single car has passed. We are the only ones out here.

Except in the distance, where a coyote howls low. The sound makes me shiver and I rub my bare upper arms.

I approach the cross, looking at the ground. "I guess we're here," I say. I search the grass, half-expecting to see blood stains. There's nothing but the usual weeds and stones of a country roadside. I'm not sure if I'm relieved or disappointed. Besides the tiny white cross, this spot is so ordinary. We could be on any stretch of road. It seems there should be more to mark the momentous event that occurred here.

Without the cross, this could be any place, nothing special.

In my mind, it is the site where my whole life changed.

I push my bangs out of my face and turn to Sawyer.

"Now what?" he asks.

"When I did this with Rylan, we held hands and she said some words."

He steps to me and takes both my hands. His palms are damp, or maybe mine are.

"What words do we say?" he asks.

"I think she prays."

"Okay." He shifts his weight from foot to foot.

I bow my head and take a moment to form the words. "Lord, let Justin come to us. Let him say what he needs to say." I feel the words are inadequate but hope they'll do the trick.

I close my eyes and focus on the quiet around us. The air feels electric, a tiny shiver in the air. I start to think this might work.

A car rushes down the highway, buffeting us with wind as it passes. My eyes fly open in surprise and fear. I had been so intent on what we were doing I didn't hear the car approaching.

"Maybe we should get a little further off the road," Sawyer says and leads me a few steps into the weeds.

Resettled, we try again. I grip his hands tightly and he squeezes back. "He has to be here," I whisper.

"I think he is," he whispers back.

My arms break out in goosebumps. "I think I feel him too," I whisper. I repeat the short prayer.

A breeze swirls around us, lifting my hair, chilling my skin. I focus harder. "Justin, are you here?" I ask the breeze.

The breeze swirls for a long moment, surrounding us in a vortex of electricity. Then it disappears as suddenly as it started. The electricity in the air disperses as well.

We're just two people on the side of the road holding hands in the moonlight.

I open my eyes and find Sawyer looking at me. "Was he here?" he asks.

"I think so." Holding hands seems silly now, so I drop mine to my sides.

"Is that how it happens with Rylan?"

"No. She can see them clearly, talk to them. It's a whole different thing."

Sawyer seems disappointed. "So we need her."

"Looks that way." I gaze over the fields, trying not to let my own disappointment show. "It was a long shot, either way."

"I did feel something. That breeze, the tingle in the air."

I'm suddenly chilled and wrap my arms across my chest. "That was something, I guess. Not sure what I expected."

He sees I'm getting cold. "Let's go back. I think we've done all we can for tonight." He places a hand on my shoulder and leads me to the vehicle.

Once back in the SUV, he says with a small smile, "That was pretty cool."

"We didn't even see anything," I say, daring to smile back just a little.

"Yeah, but normally I go to work then come home. Maybe watch some TV and then go to bed. This supernatural stuff is way out of the norm for me. It's kind of fun."

"I hear you. I'm up early to work at the donut shop and don't do much afterwards. The Hole is pretty much my entire world. Of course, I have George."

"He's great," he says, then turns thoughtful and quiet and watches the fields slide by. Soon, we are driving down the lane to my house. Only then does he talk again. "Valerie, would you like to have dinner sometime?" he blurts suddenly.

I'm surprised by the offer and my first instinct is to refuse. Then I look at his face lit by the dashboard. He looks like the friend I knew—helpful, hopeful. The idea of dinner with the man seems lovely.

"I think I'd like that."

"It wouldn't be too weird?"

"We just tried to talk to a ghost. I think dinner is the less weird thing of the two."

He chuckles a little. "I suppose you're right. I'll call you tomorrow and we can finalize the details."

"Sounds good," I say.

He reaches for the door handle as I turn off the engine. The cab grows dark until he opens his door. Then the overhead light hurts my eyes.

"Until then," I say and open my door too. I feel nervous and silly. I'm not used to the feeling, and it feels kind of good.

He goes to his car, opens his door, then turns. "I had a really nice time tonight, even if it didn't work out."

"Me too." I'm shocked to see I mean it. It's been a strange night, but a good one.

"Good luck with your missing friend."

I had forgotten about Mickey and I instantly feel guilty. "Thank you."

"You don't think the same person that hurt that girl they found at Declan's took her do you?"

"I hadn't thought of that."

And now, as he leaves and I go to bed, it's all I can think of.

TWENTY-EIGHT

RYLAN FLYNN

Soft shadows drape the kitchen as the sun begins to rise, the sky smeared in shades of pink. I listen to the coffee maker spurt and sputter. The thing is old. I bought it used at a garage sale about a year ago. Pretty sure it's on its last leg.

I think I have another one or two buried in the house somewhere. I scan the pile smothering the dining table and debate digging for it.

I'd rather do anything than worry about Mickey, and the distraction of hunting for lost treasure in my collections is enticing. But also overwhelming. I leave the search for another day and pour a cup of coffee into a to-go mug. Letting myself out the back patio door, I step into the morning.

Once outside, I realize I don't know where I'm going or what I can do to find her. I only know I can't stay here and do nothing.

When I'm seated in my car, I take out my phone and call the one person that might help.

It sounds like I've woken Ford up when he answers. I only slept a few hours curled up on Mom's bed, and it hasn't been that long since he left this driveway. I instantly feel bad for bothering him.

"I'm sorry. I didn't think about it being so early," I say.

I hear the rustle of blankets and picture him sitting up in bed to talk. "It's okay," he says. "My alarm is going to go off in a bit anyway. What's up?" There's a note of hope in his voice. "Did you hear from Mickey?"

"No. I haven't heard anything. I was hoping you had. There hasn't been a ransom notice or any word from the man who took her?"

"Not that I know of, and I doubt someone wouldn't call me immediately if there had."

My almost decent mood sinks. "That's not good is it? No ransom. He doesn't intend to return her, does he?"

Ford sighs audibly, then says, "Too soon to tell. We have to keep up the hope she'll come back."

I stare at the closed garage door growing brighter as the sky lightens. I wonder if the cat I saw the other night will make an appearance. "Hope is all we have, but the reality is she's in trouble."

"Don't go down that road," he warns. "We have to keep cool heads."

"I need to do something. I'm literally in my car ready to go, but I don't have anywhere to drive to." I sound miserable even to myself.

"Rylan, I know you want to help, but leave this to the police."

"But I have to do something. What can I do?"

"I don't know. Pray?"

That gives me an idea and a destination. I start the car. "You'll let me know if you hear anything? Anything at all."

"Of course."

I hang up and put the car in reverse. Last night, I had Mom to soothe me. Today I need Dad.

Dad's house is the only one on the block with a porch light on. He always leaves it shining all night, all day. He started it when we were younger and going out with friends at night. He didn't ever want us to come home to a dark house, so he left it on all the time. When he and Mom split and he moved to this house, he turned the light on and left it on for us.

I appreciate the light this morning, although the sun is fully up by the time I park in his driveway. It makes me feel like I've come home.

Besides the porch light, however, it looks like the house is dark. I doubt he is up yet, so I sit on the front step with my coffee and wait, fiddling with the lid on my to-go cup. I watch as the neighborhood wakes up and people start getting into cars, going to work or school. It seems strange to me that life is going on around me as usual, when I feel my world has been torn apart by Mickey's abduction.

I can only imagine the torture Marco is going through.

Eventually, I can't take it anymore, can't sit still. I stand and knock on Dad's front door before I walk in calling, "Dad, it's Rylan."

The silence of the house is so complete a frizzle of fear shoots down my back. Is it too quiet? Normally, Dad has the TV on or a radio or some sort of background noise. All I can hear is the tick of a clock.

"Dad?" I call again, all sorts of scenarios bubbling in my head. Most of them ending badly.

I make my way down the hall toward his bedroom at the end. I've rarely come this far into the house and I feel like I'm trespassing now.

When I reach the door at the end of the hall, I knock softly. "Dad? You up?"

He doesn't answer immediately and my overworked mind jumps to the worst possible scenario. I tell myself I'm being silly. Dad is probably just still in bed. But my mind won't quit.

I knock harder, more insistent. "Dad?" I shout. "You in there?"

The door opens suddenly and Dad stands there wearing shorts and a rumpled t-shirt, his thinning hair sticking up all over. "Rylan, what in the world?" He sounds irritated. I'm so relieved he's okay, I don't mind the grumble.

"I thought maybe something happened to you," I blurt.

He glances over his shoulder to the clock on the night stand. "Why are you here so early? Is everything okay?" His face is heavy with worry.

"No, everything is not okay."

"Keaton?"

"Not Keaton," I assure him. "It's Mickey. She's been taken."

Standing in the doorway, I explain what happened. "Will you pray with me? Pray she comes home."

"Of course," he says, rubbing his face. "Just give me a minute to wake up and take this all in."

"I'll wait in the kitchen."

In the kitchen, I press the start button on his coffee maker. As usual, he set it before going to bed. His maker is much quieter than mine, and soon the kitchen is full of the smell of fresh coffee.

"Okay," Dad says, coming into the kitchen in a fresh shirt and slacks. He's combed his hair and he looks more like the pastor he is. "Tell me everything. You sure she didn't just go out or something?"

I press my lips together in agitation and shake my head. "There were broken things in the house. She obviously fought back. Her computers and stuff were smashed, too."

He looks thoughtful as he pours the coffee into his "World's Best Dad" mug I bought him in middle school. The bright orange letters seem out of place with my dark mood.

"So she was taken. Do the police have any leads or ideas?"

"I just talked to Ford and they don't have anything." My

voice cracks as I sit at the dining table. "I'm so scared, Dad. She has to be okay."

"She will be," he says, with so much conviction I want to believe him. "God will look after her."

"But God let her be taken in the first place," I counter. I get a sudden flash of memory, of me saying these same words to Dad after Mom was murdered. The memory makes me uncomfortable. This has to turn out differently. It's too late for Mom, but not for Mickey.

"God's plan is so far beyond our comprehension," he replies, unfazed, joining me at the table. He sits the mug down and takes my hands in his. "Do you want to pray for her now?"

I squeeze his hands and bow my head.

"Lord, please look after Mickey. Put a hedge of protection around her," he starts. I close my eyes and listen intently to his words as he continues. After a while, the words lull my frayed nerves. Almost like magic, I feel a peace seep into me, my muscles relaxing, my mind calming.

Several minutes later, when he says *amen*, I flutter my eyes open and hold onto his hands. "Thank you," I whisper.

"She will be found," he assures me, squeezing my hands then letting go.

I sit back in my chair and take a sip of my coffee. It has grown cold, so I go to the maker to top it off. "Keaton was at the scene last night," I say as I spoon sugar into my cup.

"Is he assigned to the case?"

"I guess so. He wasn't too happy to see me there and he let me know it."

When I turn around, Dad is grinning. "You two have always been like oil and water. If you would learn to work together, things would be easier for you both."

I want to say it's all Keaton's fault, but I know that's not true, so I change the subject. "Mickey's house is haunted," I say.

"Really?" Dad grows excited, quickly grasping the implications. "So there might be a witness?" I love that he understands and accepts.

"I tried to talk to the little boy. He is very weak and didn't stay long. All he said was that it was a dark man."

Dad drinks his coffee, thinking.

"Dark? Like skin or hair or what?"

"I think as in his spirit or whatever. A darkness in the man. But I can't be sure."

"That isn't easy to track down."

"I wasn't much help," I say.

"Maybe not last night. But you could try again."

"It's a crime scene so I couldn't go in the house. I was only allowed in the side yard."

"Like that's stopped you before," he scoffs.

"He's so weak and scared. I'm not sure if he has anything useful to say, even if I could talk to him again."

"Too bad Mickey is the one missing. You always have good luck when she's there with you. You two are a good team."

"*Were* a good team. She was taking a break from the show before she was taken. She thought being with me was too dangerous. I can't imagine what she'll feel about it after she comes home. As long as she comes home, I don't care if she ever does the show again."

"You will find her."

"Me? There's nothing I can do. The little boy is beyond my reach and I have no idea where to look for her."

"Maybe he won't talk to you alone, but if you had some help." He eyes me over the rim of his cup.

"No offense, Dad, but I don't think he'll talk to you either."

"I don't mean me. What about that Jamie you met, the house rehabber? You said she could hear the spirits. If you teamed up, maybe he will be able to say more."

I start to warm to the idea. "That might work," I say, excited.

"Maybe he can give us a description or something useful this time."

"Now you're thinking."

I grab my coffee then kiss Dad on the cheek. "I have to go."

Finally, some way I can help.

TWENTY-NINE

FORD PIERCE

After last night's almost kiss and this morning's wake-up call, I find it hard to push Rylan out of my head. Her lips keep floating through my mind and I feel an odd mix of attraction and disgust at myself.

"She's only Keaton's sister," I grumble as I drive to work. I can't believe that old line anymore. Something has shifted in our relationship. She's no longer the skinny kid that followed us around. She hasn't been for a long time.

As I park my car in the lot at the precinct, I take a long breath. "Think about that later," I say out loud. "You have to find Mickey today."

That sobers me. I feel guilty for thinking of kisses when I should be totally focused on my missing friend.

I'd hoped that a few hours of sleep would help with ideas to find her, but I'm still at a loss. This isn't a normal missing person's case. We usually start with the family and friends of the victim, hoping they are just hiding out somewhere. The scene clearly shows that Mickey didn't leave of her own will. She's not hiding out. She's being hidden.

Ashby may be a small town, but there are still plenty of places to hide her.

As I walk through the parking lot, a middle-aged couple hurries for the sidewalk, passing me. The man walks stiffly, angry. The woman clings to his arm. It's obvious she's been crying. I've only met Mickey's parents once before, but I remember Mrs. Bartlett's curly dark hair, so like her daughter's.

Mickey's parents have come home from Florida to find her.

I have the irrational urge to get back in my car and drive away instead of facing the mother's fear and the father's anger. I straighten my back and catch up to them.

"Mr. and Mrs. Bartlett?" I ask when in earshot.

Mr. Bartlett looks over his shoulder and stops when he recognizes me. "Pierce," he says shortly, stopping on the sidewalk.

"We were just coming to see you," Mrs. Bartlett says. "Any news?"

Her face is so full of hope I hate to crush it. "Sorry, nothing yet."

"Well, she didn't just disappear into thin air. You have to find her," her husband says.

I don't take his anger personally. "Let's go inside to my office. Detective Spencer should be in now. We can all talk together."

"Fine," he says. "Lead the way."

When we enter the office, the lights are off. Tyler isn't in yet.

"Where's the other detective?" Mrs. Bartlett asks in a thin voice.

"He'll be here any minute," I say. "Please take a seat, Mrs. Bartlett."

"Jeanie," she says.

"Right, Jeanie. Would you like some coffee? It's not the best but it is wet and hot."

"We don't want coffee," Mr. Bartlett says. "We want Mickey home."

"That's what we all want," I say.

An uncomfortable silence fills the tiny room. My head is thick and heavy from lack of sleep and I really want a coffee to help clear it. I'm debating leaving the room for one when Tyler finally arrives.

He looks from me to the Bartletts. "Hello?"

"Tyler, these are Mickey's parents, the Bartletts."

Tyler says hello and shakes hands.

"So sorry about Mickey. She's wonderful," Tyler says, more at ease than I feel.

"You know her?" Jeanie asks.

"I do." Tyler darts a look at me, wondering how much to give away. "We've worked with her a little."

"Oh, she told me all about that," Jeanie beams. "She was so proud to be part of solving a crime."

"She was a big help," I say.

Mr. Bartlett gives me a stern look. "Do you normally use ghost hunters in your work?" I gather from his tone that he doesn't like the idea.

"We use whatever will help solve the case," I say, trying not to grow defensive. The man is in a bad way, after all.

"Mickey and Rylan have been an asset to us," Tyler says smoothly. "More than once."

"Rylan has always led Mickey into trouble. I wouldn't be surprised if her kidnap leads back to Rylan in some way," Michael says.

I bristle at this and open my mouth to protest.

"I'm sure that's not the case," Jeanie intervenes. "Rylan has always been a good friend to Mickey. This is not her fault in any way."

The words seem to calm Michael. "Maybe not," he grumbles. "So, what are you doing to find my daughter?" he asks, pinning me down with his gaze.

"We, uh—" I flounder at the direct question.

"That's what I thought," he says. "Here's the thing, your department is not equipped to handle her case. I've already called the state police."

"You called them?" Tyler asks, dumbfounded.

"I did. I have a friend at the state level. I called in a favor."

"I'm sure we can handle this," I protest.

"If you could, you would have already. She's been missing for hours and you have nothing," Michael says.

"We're doing all we can."

"That's why you were just getting here when we arrived? You should have been out all night looking."

I'm starting to get angry and, honestly, a little guilty. We've been running ragged working the Skylar Chrisman case. When I went to bed early this morning, I was beat. I desperately needed the few hours rest to be fresh this morning.

I don't tell the Bartletts that. They wouldn't understand and I don't blame them.

"You said you'd use whatever will help the case. The state boys have a lot more resources than you do. Use them."

I can't argue the point, so I keep my mouth shut, although it rankles.

"I'm sure we'd love to have help from the state police," Tyler says, smoothing over the tension in the room. "We just have to clear it with Chief McKay."

"Already talked to him, too. The detectives will be here this morning. It's all taken care of."

I sit taller in my seat, angry at his going over our heads. I again open my mouth, but when Jeanie gives me a pained look, I swallow the harsh words I want to say. "I'm sure we will all work together nicely," I say tightly. It's the best I can do at the moment.

"You're busy with the case of that murdered girl that Rylan got Mickey mixed up in," Michael says. Again with the bashing of Rylan. I've had about as much as I can take of that.

I remind myself that he's under a tremendous amount of stress right now and force my shoulders to relax a little.

"We are working that case as well," Tyler interjects. "I'm sure the state police will be a wonderful asset in finding Mickey. That's all that really matters."

Chief McKay suddenly ducks his head into our office. He rarely comes down here himself. Judging by the tight set of his lips, he's not happy to be here. He glances at the Bartletts, his eyes lingering a hard moment on Michael. Chief McKay then nods at the man and he nods back.

"Pierce and Spencer," Chief says. "Can you come with me a moment?"

We stand dutifully and follow the chief into the hall. "I'm guessing this is about the state police coming," I say.

"So he told you. Look, this is out of my hands. It's probably for the best. You are both too close to the victim in this."

"We don't have to like it," I say.

"No, but you do have to step down. The state investigators are already here. I expect you to work well with them. Give them anything they need."

"You know we will," Tyler says. "Whatever it takes."

"Anything they need," I add.

"Good, because here they come." McKay steps back and a man and woman dressed in suits walk down the hall toward us. I feel a little underdressed in my polo-shirt uniform.

The woman smiles as they join us, but the man is more reserved. "You must be Pierce and Spencer," she says looking us over and offering her hand. She has a large birthmark on one cheek. My eyes are drawn to the maroon splotch, but I hastily look away. She sees me looking and her lips press together a moment.

Tyler takes her offered hand first. "I'm Spencer," he shakes her hand, not seeming to notice the birthmark.

"Erin Emery," she says and gives him one strong shake before releasing and reaching for me. Her hand is strong and sure in mine, a question in her eyes, almost a dare. Then I notice a little softness at the eyes and a slight uptick at the corners of her mouth that might pass as a smile.

"Don't worry, you can look at it," she says drily.

"I'm Pierce," I say, feeling foolish, looking her directly in the eyes, ignoring her comment.

The man with her reaches for my hand. "Davis Jorgenson," the man says with a heavy southern accent. "Pleased to meet ya both." Jorgenson lets go of my hand and fiddles with his bright, colorful tie. The multi-colored dots are a stark contrast to his dark suit.

"Nice to meet you, Emery and Jorgenson," McKay says, getting in on the hand shaking. "Welcome to Ashby."

Emery pushes a piece of her short hair behind her ear and addresses McKay. "Is there somewhere we can work from? I'd like to sit down with the case and get started."

"You can use the conference room for now," McKay says. "I'm sure Pierce and Spencer will get you up to speed."

"That would be great," Jorgenson drawls.

"Of course. We'll be right there," I say and let McKay lead them to the small conference room down the hall.

When they're gone, I exchange a look with Tyler. "Guess we're off Mickey's case."

"Looks like it." We both stare down the hall. "Think they'll find her?" Tyler gives voice to my fears.

"They better."

THIRTY

RYLAN FLYNN

Jamie doesn't answer when I call so I have to leave a message. How do you leave a message about contacting a dead boy? I said "please call back it's kind of urgent" and left it at that.

I sit in my car in front of Dad's, clutching my phone, waiting for Jamie to call, when Aunt Val does instead.

"Any news?" she asks.

"Nothing yet." I then tell her about my plan to try to contact the little boy again.

She's quiet a moment when I finish explaining. "Sounds like you have things under control then."

I scoff out loud. "Not at all. I'm just flailing around looking for any way to help. I just realized you called a few times and I missed it. I'm sorry."

She's quiet again and I get the feeling she has something she wants to tell me. "Everything okay?" I ask.

"Yes. It's just... I don't want to add to your plate, but, last night, Sawyer and I tried to contact Justin."

I'm surprised. "Holy flip! You did? How'd it go?"

"We went to the scene of the accident and called to him. The wind blew a little, but that's it."

"Okay, that's cool. Wish I could have helped, but—"

"No, I totally get it. I shouldn't have even said anything." She pauses again. "Can I ask something?" She sounds afraid of my answer.

"Of course."

"Do you think it would be wrong to go out with Sawyer? Like on a date?"

This is not what I thought she'd ask. I've never known Val to date. I like the idea, though. "Do you want to?"

"He asked me and I said yes. Now I'm wondering if it is too weird with our history and all."

"I think you should look for happiness wherever it comes from. Your history might just bring you together."

My phone chirps that I have another call. It's Jamie. "Look. I have a call I have to take, but I say go for it."

I say a quick goodbye and switch to Jamie.

She seems surprised to hear from me, but it doesn't take much explanation to get her to understand what I want to do and why I need her.

"I could use the help."

"Why do you need me?"

"You have a gift too. You can hear the spirits. I need everyone I can get to help find Mickey."

She hesitates a moment, then says, "I'm in."

I tell her where and when.

I have some time to fill before she'll get to Mickey's and I spend it driving around the outskirts of town, places I didn't drive last night. I search the roadsides and the field edges as I drive. I'm not sure what I hope to find. Finding Mickey's body is too horrible to think of. Still, I look. I don't know what else to do.

I see a lot of cows, but no Mickey.

I finally give up and head to her house.

The yellow tape is still up and the sight of it is jarring in the bright sun.

Jamie's truck is already here. We meet on the sidewalk, just this side of the tape.

"Oh, man. This looks bad," Jamie says, touching the tape with a fingertip. "It makes it real, you know. Poor Mickey."

"It's real," I say sadly. I look at her seriously. "Thank you for coming. I can only hope with both of us here the ghost will be stronger and can say more."

"Where do you want to do this?" Jamie asks, nervously running a hand over her red ponytail.

I glance around the neighborhood, conscious of Mrs. Tamaka so close and possibly watching.

"Let's go around the side yard. That's where I talked to him last night."

She follows me around the property line to the side yard.

"Here's as good as any place, I guess," I say. We're only a few yards from the side of the house. I glance at the neighbor's. We're technically on their property. A dog looks out a window, but I don't see any people. It's as close to privacy as we'll get.

"This will have to work," I say. "Let's hold hands and focus. He's very weak and it's daylight, but maybe we can coax him out."

Jamie's hands are calloused and strong. I squeeze them both and she squeezes back.

"What do we do?" she asks.

"I'm going to try calling to him," I whisper. "Hey, little boy I saw last night. Please come to us again."

I open my eyes and look at Jamie questioningly. Nothing happens for several moments.

Then the dog in the window starts barking, startling me. A shimmer is forming next to us.

"I think he's here," I whisper.

"I don't see anything," Jamie whispers.

"He's faint, just a shimmer."

Jamie looks around, then closes her eyes again.

"Hello," I say gently. "I'd like to talk to you again."

The boy is nothing more than a shadow, but I can make out the outline of his angled, broken arm.

"Hello," he says, barely a whisper.

Jamie's head flies up and her eyes pop open.

"What was that? Was that him?"

"He's here," I say. "I'd like to ask you about what happened to Mickey here yesterday."

"The bad man?" he asks.

Jamie blinks fast and nods that she can hear him.

"Yes, the bad man. Can you tell me what he looks like?"

The boy raises his hands to his face. "A dark man. So much black."

"Okay, a Black man?"

"No. Just a lot of dark."

He's not making sense so I move on. "Anything else. Was he tall, short, heavy?"

"Tall." He says. His shape grows dimmer, flicks away then comes back more clearly.

"Did he say anything?" Jamie asks.

He shakes his head. "No."

"He didn't say anything at all?" I clarify.

"Just hit her and broke things."

I flinch at this.

"What was he wearing?" I ask.

"Clothes."

No help there.

"Anything at all you can tell us?" My voice raises in desperation. This isn't going anywhere.

"Is his hair dark or light?" Jamie asks, her eyes tight shut, listening intently.

"Dark hair," he seems excited. "Face hair."

"A beard," Jamie whispers. "He had a dark beard."

Finally, something useful.

"What in the world is going on here?" Harsh words from a woman's voice I don't recognize interrupt us. Jamie jumps and drops my hand. The little boy disappears.

I turn and a suited woman with a large birthmark trudges along the property line toward us.

A man in a suit and bright tie follows. I don't recognize either of them.

"I think we're in trouble," Jamie says.

I turn toward the man and woman and try for authority. "Can I help you?"

The woman stops and puts her hands on her hips in agitation. "Help us? Want to tell me what you both are doing at a crime scene?"

I feel Jamie next to me, her presence making me bold. "We're not in the scene." I point to the tape between us and the house. "We're on this side."

"That doesn't explain what you're doing."

I'm growing angry at the woman's attitude. The man behind her just watches, but I see a small twinkle of humor in his face.

"We don't need to tell you anything." I lift my chin in defiance.

The woman pulls the edge of her jacket back, showing me a badge. It's different than the one Ford wears. I lean in and read, *State Police.* "Detectives Emery and Jorgenson. We're on this case now."

Oh no.

"I'm sorry," I instantly backpedal. "I didn't realize who you were."

"We're just trying to help," Jamie adds.

"And yet you still haven't answered my question. What are you doing here?"

I reach my hand out. "I'm Rylan Flynn. I'm Mickey's best friend."

Detective Emery looks at my hand but doesn't take it.

"And her business partner? That Rylan?"

"Yes."

The woman glances at the man who still hasn't said a word. She runs her eyes down me, taking in every detail of my t-shirt and skinny jeans. Her eyes skip over Jamie dressed in work jeans, boots and a t-shirt. "Please tell me this doesn't have to do with ghosts or any such nonsense."

Detective Jorgenson makes a small chuckling sound.

"We're trying to contact the little boy spirit that is here," I say.

She nods, but I know she doesn't believe me. "A little boy? Okay. I'll play along. What did this little boy say?"

"The man that took Mickey had a dark beard," Jamie says.

"He said that?" The male partner finally speaks up with a heavy southern accent. He sounds sincerely interested.

"Yes," Jamie says. "I heard him."

Emery can barely hide her smile. "I'm sure you did. Look, I'd like to get statements from you all, and we will. But for now, I need you to get off the property. This is no place for your shenanigans."

"Look, we're only trying to help," Jamie says again, growing angry at Emery's attitude.

Emery gives her a stern look. "We don't need this kind of help."

"Time to go," Jorgenson says, stepping between us and the house. "And don't ya'll come back unless you want us to take you in."

There's nothing else to do except walk away. They follow us to our cars. Jamie gives me a sorry smile as she climbs into her truck and drives away. I hesitate by my door.

"Something else?" Emery asks. "We need you to leave."

"You will follow up on the detail of him having a beard,

right? The boy made it sound like it's a big beard. He said a 'dark face man.'"

The detectives exchange a look of disbelief. "We'll follow all legitimate leads," Emery says.

"Good. Thank you. I'll talk to you later." I climb in my car and drive away. I'm almost home before it sinks in that she said "legitimate." They have no intention of looking for a bearded man.

THIRTY-ONE

RYLAN FLYNN

As tired as I am, there's no way I can go inside my house and lie down. I feel all at loose ends. I have a burning desire to find Mickey, but nowhere to go, no direction to head in.

With nothing else to do, I return to searching the roads of Ashby and the surrounding countryside. A one-woman search party.

I drive until my eyes are blurry from searching the roadsides. I've long finished my coffee and a can of warm Dr. Pepper I found on the back seat. After all that liquid, my bladder is growing uncomfortable.

And I'm a long way from a public restroom. Just when I'm seriously contemplating squatting behind a tree, I realize I'm close to the Krieger Mansion.

Declan will let me use his restroom. It's better than the tree alternative.

At least I hope so.

I crunch down the gravel drive, under the trees lining either side. I search the windows for any sign of the ghost I saw here before. Nothing.

The smell of the lilacs is still strong when I climb out after parking behind the gardener's blue flatbed truck. It's the only vehicle out front and I wonder if Declan is even home.

I knock on the heavy wooden door and Evie barks inside. I'm almost dancing with my need for a restroom, and press my legs together in desperation.

"Holy flip, please hurry," I grumble.

I knock again and hear Evie scraping on the other side of the door. I just about give up and hurry around the corner of the house in shame when the door slides open a few inches.

Declan looks out through the gap, his eyes widening in surprise when he sees me bouncing on his front steps.

"Rylan?" He pulls the door open wider.

"Can I use the restroom?"

He steps back to let me in. "Of course. It's right down that hall."

I rush where he pointed and just make it.

When I'm done, I stare in the mirror a moment, feeling more foolish than I have in a long time. Only a child has bathroom accidents. Of course, a child wouldn't have been driving for hours.

I take a deep breath and open the bathroom door to face Declan, who is waiting in the expansive front entrance.

"I'm so sorry," I say. "I've been driving around looking for Mickey and I guess I didn't notice I had to go until it was too late."

"Don't worry about it. I'm actually glad to see you. It's awful, what happened to Mickey. Has there been any news?"

"Nothing. It's like she just disappeared into thin air." I think about what the little boy ghost said about a beard, but I keep that to myself. I don't want to explain how I got that information.

"Is there anything I can do? Any way I can help?" he asks, his voice tender.

"There's nothing. I don't even have anything to do. I've

been driving up and down the roads hoping to see her. It's a crazy thing to do, but I can't sit still."

"It's not crazy. It's only human to want to look, to try to help."

The futility of what I've been doing sinks in. "I'm only one person. We need everyone looking. Need to beat down every door until we find her."

"I don't think that's possible," he says gently, his accent thick, reaching for my hand.

I feel tears threatening, weakness and worry filling my legs, so I let him squeeze my hand.

The softness of his fingers is familiar. All the times we watched movies hand in hand flash through my mind. He is so close I can feel the heat of his body near mine. That memory is familiar too.

I don't want the memories. I don't want this man. Especially not now.

When I look up, there's a spark in his eyes that I also remember. The air crinkles with tension. It feels wrong and I drop his hand.

He seems to collect himself. "I'm sure she'll show up," he says, turning away, looking down to Evie at his feet.

"If this was one of your books, what would you do to find her?"

He smiles. "This isn't a book."

"But if it was, what should be my next step?"

"My books are from the killer's point of view, so she would never be found."

I feel like he slapped me. "That wasn't nice."

He seems instantly contrite. "I'm sorry, but you asked. If I was writing a different kind of book, I'd say keep looking. She could be close and you can't give up."

This soothes me a little. "I think I'm a touch sensitive at the moment."

"Of course you are. This is horrible."

"You have no idea."

"I'm shook up and I don't know her nearly as well as you. How are you holding up?"

"I honestly don't know." I run my hand through my hair. "I'm losing it a little."

"You look like you're keeping it together fairly well." Again, that tension just below the surface. Is he trying to flirt with me? Now of all times?

"Have you heard from Ford about the woman that died here?" I feel the need to say Ford's name and it's the only way I can think of.

Declan blinks three times before answering. "I don't think he'd tell me if there was news." There's a tightness to his words. "Besides, isn't he busy looking for Mickey?"

"True." I'm feeling nervous now and find myself playing with the charms on my bracelet. Declan sees and takes hold of my wrist gently, looking at the charms.

"Do you remember when I gave this one to you?" He takes the rainbow charm in his fingers. I had honestly not thought of it in a long time. Each charm is from some important moment in time. He gave me the rainbow charm on our one-month anniversary. I'd thought it cute, but looking back it seems sort of silly to celebrate such a small thing.

"I remember. I guess I forgot it was on there."

"Now who's not being nice?" he half teases. "You were excited to get it at the time."

"I thought differently about a lot of things then." I'm not liking the direction of this conversation. I reach for the charm. "Do you want it back?"

He seems offended. "Of course not. I like thinking that it's been on there with you this whole time."

I make a mental note to remove the charm as soon as possible. I look toward the door, ready to leave. "I think I better get going. I want to keep looking for Mickey."

He bows his head a little. "Of course. Do you want some company?"

I really don't. This whole visit has gone wrong and I just want to leave. "No. I'm good. I'm meeting with her parents in a while." It's a lie, but also a good idea. I should stop in and see them.

"Okay. Let me know when they find her. I'm really worried about her."

"I will." Another lie. I don't intend to talk to him again if I can help it. There's just too much history and something simmering below the surface that I don't want to look too closely at. That past needs to stay in the past.

I pull the heavy wooden door open, letting myself out into the late afternoon sunshine. "Thanks again for the bathroom," I say, thinking my mom would be proud I remembered my manners.

"Leaving so soon, Rylan?" a woman's voice calls down the stairs.

I look up and see Anita the housekeeper watching us. I wonder how long she has been there.

"I just stopped by." I don't want to tell her I needed a bathroom. I'm aware of how odd that makes me look. "It's nice to meet you," I add, since the first time she saw me she basically shut the door on me.

"Yes, it is nice." She ascends a few steps but still looks down on me. I get the distinct feeling she's enjoying the slight upper hand. "You really should visit more often. I'd love to get to know you better. I've heard so much about you and your show."

"I'd like that too," I say.

"I'm sorry I didn't talk to you last night. I was so shook up by what happened I didn't want to speak to anyone."

"I understand. It is all very disturbing."

"Imagine a woman dying here." She gives a visible shake. "Yikes." She comes to the bottom of the steps. "You really should visit again when all this business is over."

I'm curious why she's acting like the lady of the house, but Declan doesn't seem to notice.

"Yes, come by any time." Declan leans against the door frame after scooping Evie into his arms.

"I need to go. Mickey's parents are waiting for me." Another lie.

I give them a little wave and get in my car quickly.

As I drive down the lane, I again search for the ghost I saw before. I didn't get any tingles from her or another spirit on this visit either. All the windows are still clear and my back is silent.

THIRTY-TWO

FORD PIERCE

After Tyler and I get Detectives Emery and Jorgenson up to speed on Mickey's case, I feel empty. There wasn't much to give them.

The canvas of the neighbors didn't turn up anything useful. Everyone was either not home at the time of her abduction or they didn't see anything that might help. The broken computers might mean something. Our tech department is recovering the hard drives, hoping to find something that might lead to a suspect. Maybe she was having an affair that went wrong.

I can't imagine that being the case. Mickey and Marco always seemed to be dedicated to each other. In this business, you can't rule anything out. It will take some time to go through the computers. The state detectives didn't seem to think it would lead anywhere and I agreed.

That left us with the actual scene. Another zero. Besides some long dark hairs found on the crushed coffee table, there was nothing forensically interesting. The hairs will probably lead back to Mickey. They are consistent with her curls and were most likely lost in the struggle.

After giving this little bit of information to the new team we head back to our office. I sink into my chair, despondent. I'm sure Emery and Jorgenson will do a good job of looking for Mickey, but I feel like we should all be on the case, not turning it over.

"We should be out there," Tyler grumbles, seeming to read my mind. "Not here in our office."

"I know." I pick up a pen and tap it on the desktop. "Mickey's safety has to be our top priority, not politics."

"Our top priority is the murder." Tyler flips open the Skylar Chrisman file. "I feel like we're missing something on Skylar's case. Maybe the two cases are related?"

"Maybe we should look at the mansion again. There has to be a reason she was there."

"We crawled all over it and the farms nearby. There wasn't a drop of blood or anything at all."

"So where do we go with this now?"

"Back to the victim. Let's talk to her dad again. He was so shook up the first time. Maybe there's something he's thought of since we last talked to him."

I stand, eager to work on something useful. I grab my jacket from the back of my chair. It smells like Rylan. This makes me smile.

Tyler sees it and raises his eyebrows in question. I just shake my head and say, "Let's go."

Milton Chrisman doesn't seem happy to see us. "I don't suppose you've got the monster that hurt my baby," he says when he opens the door.

"I'm sorry, but we are still working on it," I say. "That's why we're here. Wondering if you have thought of anything that might help. Any little detail might be useful."

He steps into the house and leaves us to follow. The man is

a wreck. He's unshaven and wearing the same clothes we saw him in before. My heart hurts for him.

"I don't know what you think I can tell you. I went through everything with you before." He sinks into a recliner surrounded by empty beer cans.

"We know that," Tyler says. "It might help to go over it again."

"What is there to go over? I haven't seen Skylar for nearly six months. I told you, she ran off. Couldn't take it after my Vicky died. That child was wild and I couldn't control her. What do you want from me? To tell you this is all my fault? If she had been home and not out on the streets somewhere she'd still be alive." He searches through the cans on the table next to him, finds one with some beer left in it and tips it to his lips.

"We are not saying that at all," Tyler soothes. "We're just trying to figure out how Skylar got from Fort Wayne to Ashby."

"It's not that far," Milton challenges.

"Maybe not. But it still seems a little odd. She didn't walk to the Krieger Mansion from here."

Milton turns away. An awkward silence fills the room. I scan around the walls, thinking. I spot a book shelf stuffed full of novels.

"Are you a big reader?" I ask, trying to make a connection with the man.

Milton looks at the shelves. "Those were Vicky's. She loved books. Read all kinds of things. She even took Skylar to book signings down at the mall whenever they had them."

I scan the shelf. It's mostly the usual: James Patterson, Stephen King, Colleen Hoover. Three books are on a separate shelf, and I think I recognize the titles.

I walk to the shelf and squat to see better. "Tyler, look at this," I say, excited.

"Those are the signed copies they got at the mall," Milton says, not really interested.

Tyler slips a book off the shelf and holds it up for us both to look at.

"Are these Vicky's too?" he asks.

"No, those three are Skylar's. What do the books have to do with anything?"

Tyler and I exchange a look.

I open to the title page and see the scrawled signature.

Until we meet again, Declan Rathborne.

"This can't be a coincidence," I say.

"Actually, it could be. Lots of people have his books. He's a big deal. Especially around here. Local hero and all that."

"But he met her before. He never told us that."

"He probably didn't know. He must have seen dozens of people at the signing," Tyler says. "It's probably nothing."

"Maybe." I put the book back on the shelf.

"She has several signed books. Any time an author came to Fort Wayne, Vicky would take her. The rest are in her room," Milton says.

He stands from his recliner, his knees clicking from the movement. He leads us down a hall to a room at the end.

"I never come in here," he says. "It's just like she left it the day she ran away."

The room is definitely a teenager's. Dirty clothes cover the floor. The bed is unmade. The only thing that's neat is the book shelf. Just as her dad said, there are several paperbacks lined up on the shelves. I open a few and see signatures.

"She was very proud of her collection," Milton says. "I'm kind of surprised she left it behind." He stares at the books and rubs his face. "Too heavy to carry I guess." He sounds broken.

What I thought might be a viable lead fizzles away into coincidence.

We continue to search Skylar's room but don't find anything of interest.

"Did she keep a journal?" Tyler asks. "Or a diary?"

"No. Not that I know of. Honestly, I don't think I knew my daughter at all."

"I'm sure that's not true," I try to console. "You were both grieving. You did the best you could."

"Did I?" Two desperate words.

I'm saved by my phone ringing. It's a number I don't recognize.

I answer and listen for a few moments. "Thank you for letting us know. I really appreciate it."

Tyler stares at me, his face full of questions. "That was Emery."

"And?"

"They got the computer analysis back. Mickey had a stalker."

THIRTY-THREE

RYLAN FLYNN

Going to visit Mickey's parents seems like the best thing to do right now. Mickey's mom, Jeanie, texted me that they were in town this morning. They're staying at the only hotel in Ashby, The Refinery House. The hotel's as old as the town. The new owners put a coat of paint on the two-story place, but Mickey and I have done two shows here. The paint can't cover the hotel's sordid history. We helped a murdered prostitute from the 1890s and a man who lost everything in the Great Depression then took his own life. Both crossed over without too much prodding. The two episodes are among our most viewed.

If I wasn't so upset about Mickey, there would be no way I'd go to the hotel. We could make our whole careers on the ghosts populating the hotel. Even in the parking lot, I can feel them. I debate going in to see Jeanie and Michael or just driving away.

My back is tingling something fierce, but I go inside anyway. Her parents deserve my support.

I keep my eyes on the worn carpet as I make my way down the hall toward their room. Out of the corner of my eye, I see moving shapes that I know are not from this world, but I do my best to ignore them and knock on the Bartletts' door.

Jeanie opens right away, a hopeful look on her face. The look disappears when she sees me.

"Rylan, hi, honey. Sorry, for a crazy minute I thought you'd be Mickey." She steps back so I can enter the room full of furniture as old and worn as the carpet. Michael sits in a wingback chair in the corner and doesn't stand when I come in.

"Michael, Rylan is here," Jeanie says.

Michael looks up, his face full of clouds. "So, you dare to show your face, do you?"

I'm shocked by his vitriol. "I guess so. I thought maybe you'd like a visit." I'm suddenly sure this is a bad idea. Jeanie has always been nice to me. Michael, I've rarely even talked to. This unfiltered anger is a shock.

"If it wasn't for you, Mickey would be home safe," he says. "You've been nothing but trouble since she met you."

I'm temporarily stunned to silence. Then my anger rears its head. "I am not trouble. I love Mickey."

"Love her so much that you let some poor woman die in her hands?" He stands from the chair and takes a step toward me.

I hold my ground. "That was not my fault and neither is her abduction. You can't blame me."

"Can't I?" His eyes flash and he balls his hands. For a wild moment, I wonder if he will swing at me. I've never seen him like this.

Jeanie intervenes before I can find out, putting her body between ours. "Now stop that. It will not bring Mickey back."

He glares at me then turns away. "Nothing will bring her back. Don't you see?"

I finally realize he's mad at the world, at the situation. I'm just an easy target.

"Don't say that," Jeanie snaps. "She will be back. And soon. She has to." She sinks onto the bed with its light blue chenille spread. She presses her hands together in her lap.

"They will find her," I say, sitting next to Jeanie. "We have to keep the hope alive."

She turns tortured eyes to me. The whites of her eyes are red and bloodshot. I wonder when she last slept. They drove straight through from Florida last night.

"You must be exhausted," I say. "Maybe you two should get some rest. I'm sure Ford will let us know if they find anything."

"He's off the case," Michael says. "I called in the state police. Someone has to do something around here."

"I met the new team earlier. I'm sure they are working hard." I don't know what else to say, but get the feeling that defending Ford and Tyler is not the right path to take.

"They already have a viable lead." Michael sits again in the wingback chair. There is a shifting shadow behind him, but I don't think he wants to hear about that right now.

"A lead? What is it?"

"They are on their way to discuss it with us," Jeanie says. "They'll probably want to talk to you too."

I look from one to the other. "Did they say what the lead was?"

"Another way your little show got our girl in trouble," Michael says. "Did you know she had a stalker?"

I turn cold at the word. "She never said anything. Like someone was following her?"

"When they went through her computers they found a bunch of emails from a crazed fan. Said he has been watching her. The emails just got more desperate and threatening as time went on. Didn't she tell you any of this?"

I'm glad I'm already sitting or my legs would give out. "I don't read the emails. Mickey always handles that part of the business," I say vaguely, guilt sitting heavily in my belly. "This really is all my fault," I whisper.

"Now, honey, that's not true," Jeanie says. "Mickey loved doing the show with you. It was her choice."

"But if the show led to her abduction—"

"Then it's the crazed fan's fault," she finishes. I can't believe how nice Jeanie is being to me. Michael is just glaring, obviously not agreeing with his wife.

We sit in awkward silence for a moment. The spirit behind Michael's chair moves around the room, an unwanted distraction.

I'm suddenly, irrationally, angry at the shadow. Mickey got hurt because I can see spirits.

"Get out!" I scream at the shadow, jumping to my feet. "Go away and leave me alone."

Jeanie flinches and Michael seems unsurprised. I go after the shadow, waving my arms as if I'm fanning away smoke.

"Rylan, please," Jeanie says. "What are you doing?"

"There's a ghost here. There are ghosts everywhere." I feel my face growing hot and the prickle in my back growing more insistent. "This hotel is crawling with them."

I need to get out, away. I'm making an already horrible situation worse for them.

"Maybe you should leave," Michael says.

My heart is pounding and my back aches. "I'm sorry. I don't know what came over me," I try.

Jeanie gives me a pained look. "This is hard on all of us."

But hardest on them.

Miserable, I cross the room to the door. "So sorry," I say and turn the knob.

I open the door to Detective Emery's surprised face, her hand raised to knock.

"You again?" she asks.

"I was just leaving." I try to push past her.

Detective Jorgenson steps in front of me, his colorful tie at eye level. "We need to talk to you," he says.

I step back into the room and they follow. With all of us,

plus the spirit, the room feels crowded and hot. I have trouble catching my breath.

"Is this about the stalker that might have taken Mickey?" I ask.

Emery looks around the room. "They told you. Good. Now you're up to speed. Did you know about this man?"

"No, I didn't. If I had, I'd have told Ford and Tyler. Mickey probably didn't want to scare me."

Emery studies my face. "Do you have any idea who this mystery man might be?"

"I have no idea who would want to hurt Mickey. She's the sweetest."

Jorgenson brushes this away. "Someone did hurt her, so someone had it out for her. You're her best friend, she didn't tell you anything about it?"

I'm really beginning to not like this man. I shake my head.

"How about you, Mom, Dad?" he continues. "Did she tell you about the problem with this fan?"

Jeanie looks like she's about to cry. "She didn't say anything."

"You really think this guy took her?" Michael asks. "Have you tracked him down yet?"

"Tech is working on the location the emails came from. It shouldn't be long," Emery says. She studies me. "Maybe he has a beard." I can't tell if she's serious or making fun of me.

"He probably does," I defend.

"We'll find out."

I don't want to fight with the detectives. I just want Mickey back.

"Can I go? I don't know anything that I haven't already told the police."

After a long moment, Emery nods. "We'll be in touch if we need you." Her tone makes it clear that they will never need me, that I'm a nuisance.

Relieved just the same, I hurry from the room without a look back.

My back still tingles fiercely, so I keep my eyes on the faded carpet the whole way down the hall to the door. Once outside, I take a deep breath and turn my face to the sinking sun.

It's been twenty-four hours since Mickey was taken and we're no closer to finding her.

"Lord, let her be okay," I whisper to the sky.

THIRTY-FOUR

MICKEY RAMIREZ

The plastic ties cut into my wrists where they are strapped to the chair arms. I try not to pull on them, but I can't seem to help myself, even when it bites.

"That won't help you," he says, his voice altered by some machine, hard and metallic. The strange sound startles me. He hasn't said much since he took me.

My eyes are covered with a blind that is tied too tight and pulls my hair. I can only see a thin line of light at the bottom of my vision. Nothing helpful.

My mouth is dry from the gag. I desperately want to swallow, but I can't.

I pull against the ties again and scream against the gag for the hundredth time.

He laughs the metallic laugh.

I freeze, terrified by the sound.

"Please," I beg into the gag.

"Keep begging. I like that."

I stop making noise. Stop moving. He wants me to fight. I won't give him the satisfaction.

"We are going to have some fun now," he says, his voice

moving closer. I feel something touching my face, a gloved finger.

I squeeze my eyes against tears, not wanting to give him the satisfaction.

The fear consumes me as tears slide out from under the blindfold and down my cheeks.

I think of Marco. Picture his strong hands pummeling the man holding me captive.

I know he will never find me.

As the gloved finger slides to my neck, I begin to pray.

THIRTY-FIVE

RYLAN FLYNN

I can't sit in the parking lot of the hotel forever. I'm itching to drive somewhere. I want to keep looking for Mickey, but I've run out of places to look. Music plays low on the radio. "Nicotine" from Panic! at the Disco comes on and I break. It's my and Mickey's favorite song. The one we most often listen to after filming.

I flip the music off and take deep breaths until my heart stops pounding and my tears dry.

Across the parking lot, near the front door of the historic hotel, a ghost leans against the porch railing. It's an old man. He waves a friendly hello.

I put my car in reverse and drive away.

It seems like ages since I've eaten and my stomach growls ruthlessly. I soon find myself on the town square in front of The Hole. My mom would tell me a donut is not a dinner. I don't care.

"Rylan Flynn. I'm surprised to see you," an unwelcome voice calls from the steps of the courthouse across the street. Lindy Parker hurries down the steps and across the sidewalk, her high heels clicking on the concrete.

I debate ignoring her and escaping into the shop. She seems to read my intentions and raises a hand. "Wait, I wanted to talk to you."

So I wait on the sidewalk, the smell of donuts wafting through the door nearby, my mind scrambling for a reason Lindy would want to talk to me.

"Hey," I say lamely when she reaches my side. Her strong perfume battles with the smell of the bakery.

"I can't believe you're here getting donuts right now," she accuses, her fake smile tight.

"A girl's gotta eat," I try for off-handed.

"After what happened to your friend I'd imagine you'd have other things to do."

She means more important things, and she's right. "I do."

She shifts her expensive purse on her shoulder. "I'm so sorry to hear about Mickey. She was always so sweet."

"*Is* sweet. Not *was*."

Lindy blinks rapidly, her plastic smile faltering. "Of course. That's what I meant."

"We will find her," I say forcefully, stepping closer to Lindy.

"I'm sure. It's just that first you're involved in the murder of that poor girl the other night and now this thing with Mickey. Trouble really does follow you around."

I feel like she's doused me with ice water. "None of this is my fault."

Her tight smile grows wide. "Keep telling yourself that."

My hands itch to smack the smile off her face. The door to The Hole opens and Val's assistant, Eileen, steps onto the sidewalk. "Rylan, were you coming in?" She looks pointedly at my hands. I hadn't realized I'd balled them into fists. I shake them loose.

"I'm coming," I tell Eileen. "Lindy, such a pleasure as always," I say with heavy sarcasm.

I step forward, toward the door, making her flinch a little.

The tiny movement fills me with a satisfaction my mother would not be proud of.

Eileen and I leave Lindy on the sidewalk and enter the heaven-scented shop.

"The usual? One bear claw?" Eileen asks.

My stomach grumbles just then. "Make it two."

I find myself in front of Mickey's house. I know it's pointless. I know the police told me to stay away, but I can't help myself.

Staring at the front door, I let my mind turn over the few facts I have. It's pitifully little. A man with a dark beard and a mysterious stalker that I know nothing about. I can't imagine who would be stalking Mickey. They said he was watching her. Did he sit in front of her house like I am now?

Reflexively, I look around the neighborhood. No mysterious men are lurking around. In fact, the street is almost empty. The only person I can see is Mrs. Tamaka on her porch swing. No help there.

She sees me looking and smiles kindly.

I climb out of my car and walk up to her house. "Hi," I say, testing the waters. I don't know this woman and I might not be welcome.

"No news on your friend?" she asks, patting the cushion next to her.

I sink into the seat, thankful to not be alone, even if she's a stranger.

"Nothing concrete." From this vantage point, I can see all of Mickey's house and some of the alley behind. "You sure you didn't see anything?" I ask, my voice full of hope.

She thinks hard, her wrinkles growing deeper. "Nothing from the time she was taken."

"What about before that? In the morning maybe. Did you see anything out of the ordinary?"

She suddenly brightens a little. "I did see a strange truck."

I perk up. "What kind of truck?"

"An old one. The kind where the back is flat."

"A flatbed?"

"Yeah. That's what you call them. A flatbed. It was blue, I think. I remember because I hadn't seen it before and it was different than the shiny trucks I normally see around here. Most everyone seems to drive a truck nowadays."

My mind races. I know I've seen a blue flatbed recently, but can't place the memory. Of course, it might mean nothing. At least it's a tiny grain of a lead.

We sit in silence, swinging slowly, watching the sun set.

"It's so pretty out here," Mrs. Tamaka says. "Hard to believe something so bad as your friend being taken happened in this neighborhood."

"We'll find her," I say, for what feels like the fifty-third time. If I keep saying it, maybe I'll believe it.

Something niggles at the back of my mind. A blue truck and a beard. It skitters away again.

I can't sit still any longer. "Thank you for letting me sit with you," I say as I stand.

"No problem. I don't get many visitors. Good luck."

On impulse, I lean in and give her a hug. She smells like lilacs.

The memory floating at the edges of my mind suddenly clicks into place.

"I have to go," I say and hurry down the steps to my car.

I call Ford as I drive. He doesn't answer and I'm forced to leave a message. "I think I know who took Mickey." I tell him what I think happened and drive as fast as my old Caddy will take me. I queue up "Nicotine" on my phone and sing along with the song as loud as I can.

THIRTY-SIX

FORD PIERCE

I want to storm up to Emery and Jorgenson and demand details about Mickey's stalker. When we get back to the precinct they're not there. I have nowhere to storm, so I flop into my desk chair with a *humph*.

I hate being off the case. I hate not helping find Mickey. I hate that we don't know what happened to Skylar Chrisman. We've talked to her friends and family, but nothing helpful has come up. It's like she disappeared six months ago then reappeared in that garden.

"You look awful," Tyler says as he sits at his desk. "Like you're ready to punch someone."

I give him a wry smile. "I hate this. I feel so hog-tied where Mickey is concerned."

"They will find the stalker and then find her." He sounds so confident, but it doesn't make me feel better.

"If the stalker is the one who has her."

"Seems likely."

I toss a pen at him. "Stop being so reasonable."

He catches the pen in mid-air. "I can't help it. I'm a reasonable guy."

I roll my eyes, but feel better. Still frustrated, but calmer.

"Something bothers me about Skylar's case," I say, flipping her file open so I can add notes about our first visit with her dad.

"Everything about Skylar's case bothers me," Tyler says.

"Me, too. We must be missing something." I turn the pages of the file. It's pitifully thin. I shut it with a snap.

"I think we're better served trying to solve Mickey's case even if we are off it officially. Skylar is gone. We could still save Mickey."

"I'm game," Tyler says. "What are you thinking?"

"I wish I knew." I boot up my computer and open the digital file on Mickey. Not knowing where else to start, I pull up the pictures of the crime scene. There are pictures of the living room with its broken coffee table and smashed vase. There are pictures of the flipped chairs. It is hard to look at, knowing our friend was fighting for her life.

I finish by looking at the ones of her office. Her computers and video equipment are smashed and lying on the floor. I study each picture in turn, hoping to find something the techs missed.

"Tyler, look at this." I point to a detail in one picture.

"You don't think?"

We stare at each other, testing the theory in our minds.

A knock on the door interrupts us as Chief McKay ducks his head in.

"They have an address for the stalker on the Ramirez case," he says. "They are heading over there now. Do you want in?"

I'm out of the chair before he finishes the sentence. McKay hands me a slip of paper with the address on it.

I read the name on the paper. "Jared Speckler," I say to Tyler as we hurry to the car.

"Not the pig farmer?"

"The same."

We speed out of town and down country roads as the sun

drops over the fields in a blaze of pink and orange. The dark sedan Emery and Jorgenson drive is waiting at the end of the long lane leading to Speckler Farm.

"Thought you might want to be here for this," Emery says, pulling off her suit jacket and replacing it with a Kevlar vest with *state police* written across the chest.

"We appreciate it," I say, getting our vests out of the trunk of the cruiser. "You think Mickey is in there?"

"Jared Speckler has been watching Mickey, threatening her. He's our most likely suspect."

"He didn't seem like the stalker type when we talked to him before," Tyler says.

"Before?" Jorgenson asks.

I point to the woods way behind the farm. "On the other side of those trees is where Skylar Chrisman was found."

The investigators exchange looks. "Interesting," Emery says and walks faster up the drive.

The pigs in the pastures on either side follow us up the lane, snuffling at the fence in the growing dark. The farmstead is quiet as we cross the yard to the two-story traditional farm house. The house is dark, even though it's just past sunset. Speckler said he goes to bed early. Could he already be asleep?

We follow Emery single-file up the front steps to the door. She presses her face to the glass panes of the door that's as old as the house. "There's a flicker from somewhere in back," she says.

She raises a hand and pounds the police knock that's unmistakable. "State police," she shouts. "Jared Speckler, are you in there?"

I find a window on the porch and look inside the house. A shadow moves across the front room into what must be the kitchen. "He's on the move."

Sprinting down the porch steps, I hurry around the side of the house. Speckler is running for the barn, causing the motion light to click on. He looks back over his shoulder as he runs. The panicked expression is easy to see in the lights. He pulls open the man door and disappears inside the building.

All four of us give chase. I'm the first to reach the door and throw it open. "Speckler, stop. Police!" I shout into the dark of the cavernous building. I blink hard, trying to see where he went.

Tyler is right behind me, his flashlight out and panning around the open space between the haylofts. Emery and Jorgenson are right behind him, their lights out too.

"Where did he go?" she demands.

Listening closely, all I hear are the snuffles of pigs. I grab my own light from my belt and shine it toward the back of the barn. Behind a fence, several pigs stare at us, their eyes bright in the lights. Behind them some openings lead to the pastures. One or two pigs outside squeal and I hear feet pounding.

"He's in the pasture," I say, climbing the short wall between us and the pigs. I shove a few snouts away as I climb into their pen. They push their noses against my legs, curious. Tyler and the others soon follow me as I duck out the short doorways the pigs use to access the pasture.

Not too many yards away, Speckler runs under the moonlight. I sprint after him, sliding now and then on what I want to believe is mud.

Behind me, I hear Emery shout in disgust. When I look over my shoulder I see her on the ground, a stain of what probably isn't mud on the opposite side of her face as her birthmark. I turn back to Speckler and pound across the pasture.

Tyler and Jorgenson are right behind me as we close the distance to Speckler. I pound my legs harder.

"Stop, police," Jorgenson shouts half a step behind me.

Speckler keeps running across the pasture, but soon reaches the fence. He leaps on it, ready to climb over. I reach him first and grab the back of his shirt. I pull him to the ground as Tyler and Jorgenson join me.

"We told you to stop," I say as I wrestle the man's hands behind his back. He's slick with sweat and I almost lose my grip as he pulls away.

"I didn't do anything," Speckler protests.

"Then why did you run?" Emery asks, joining our group, wiping at her dirty face.

"I was scared."

"Because you kidnapped Mickey Ramirez?" I ask.

"Mickey? I didn't kidnap her. I'd never hurt her." He wriggles underneath me, pulls away as I try to put cuffs on him.

"You're as jumpy as a frog in a skillet," Jorgenson says. "Stop moving."

"Is Mickey okay?"

"You tell us. You've been watching her and emailing her," Emery says. "Makes sense you'd want more and took her."

"I'd told you I'd never hurt her. I love her."

"Love her?" Securely cuffed now, I turn him onto his back and let him sit up. "Why don't you just start from the beginning. How do you know Mickey?"

Speckler looks up, grass stuck in his hair. "I watch her show."

"She isn't on camera on the show," Tyler points out.

"She's behind the camera. What we see is what she sees. It's like being in her head."

"Except that's a show. Not the real her," I say.

"Not to me," he says miserably. "Look, I may have emailed her a few times. I may have watched her through her windows, but I did not kidnap her."

"How often do you watch her?" I demand.

"Not too much. Just every so often."

"When's the last time?" Tyler asks.

He looks down at the grass.

"You're hiding something. Spill it," Emery demands.

"I was at the Krieger the night that woman died there."

"You saw what happened? Or you had the woman captive here and followed her there when she escaped?" I ask.

His eyes grow wide. "I didn't have anything to do with that poor woman and what happened to her."

"Then why were you there?" Jorgenson asks.

"I heard that Mickey would be there, so I went to watch."

"And what did you see?" I ask.

"Nothing more than what you already know. A shadow just appeared in the back yard and fell in the garden."

"And you didn't tell us when we were here before?" Tyler asks.

"I had no way of explaining why I was there. I didn't want you to think I had anything to do with it. Look, you have to believe me. I didn't hurt that woman and I certainly didn't take Mickey."

"You've been watching her. Have you seen anything suspicious? Anything at all?"

Speckler screws his face up, thinking. "I don't know. Honestly, I didn't watch her that often. I swear."

"I don't think he knows anything," Emery says, pulling Speckler up on his feet. "We'll take it from here. Should have known he didn't have her. He's clean shaven," she says with a little laugh.

I don't understand the joke. "Clean shaven?"

"We caught Mickey's ghost hunter friend at the crime scene earlier. She said a ghost told her the kidnapper had a beard."

"Rylan told you that?" I ask.

"That girl's roof ain't nailed tight," Jorgenson drawls. "It doesn't mean anything." We lead Speckler back across the pasture to the gate. I don't like them making fun of Rylan, but I let it slide for now.

"Did you get a match on the hair found on the table at the crime scene?" I ask, thinking about the connection Tyler and I found earlier with the pictures of Mickey's office.

Emery stops and blinks at me. "We did."

"And, were they Mickey's, or could they have been beard hair?"

"They were neither."

"How do you know?"

"They were fake."

THIRTY-SEVEN

RYLAN FLYNN

It isn't until I'm driving down the tree-lined lane and see the turrets clawing at the moon that I think maybe this is a bad idea. I check my phone to see if Ford's called back and I somehow missed it. No call.

I should really call 911.

And tell them what? That I know a guy with a beard?

They'd laugh and hang up. Worse yet, they'd put me through to Emery and Jorgenson and I'd have to explain to them. I'd rather check it out myself.

When I park in front of the mansion, there's no sign of the blue flatbed truck that Declan's gardener, Keith Gillespie, drives. I did see it here. I'm sure of it. And I remember his beard as a big black bush on his face.

Now that I'm parked, the consequences of what I'm doing sink in. I can't very well just walk to the cottage and demand that he give me Mickey back. Either he'll hurt me or call the cops himself, saying a crazy woman is on his front step.

I get out of the car and shut the door as quietly as possible. There's only one lighted window in the mansion and I wonder if Declan is even home. It's better he doesn't know what I'm up to until I have some proof.

I trudge through the moonlight, careful to skirt around the garden. The large lilac bushes still fill the air with their aroma.

The trees soon swallow me as I approach the cabin.

A faint light spills through one window, maybe a nightlight in the kitchen. Now that I'm up close to the cabin, doubt surges. The place is tiny, how could he hold Mickey here? Is the fact Mrs. Tamaka saw a flatbed and the boy ghost saw a beard enough to blame the man? How many men in Ashby have beards and drive trucks?

Questions flit through my mind as I stare at the dark cabin from behind a tree.

Even though I'm fairly sure Keith Gillespie isn't home, I creep to the front window, the one with the light. Scraggly bushes grow under the window and I push through them, the branches grabbing at my skin.

Crouching under the sill, I raise until my eyes are just over the edge of the glass and peer in. Most of the cabin is one open room, the light over the sink illuminating all but the far corners. I don't see a bed and I assume the door in back leads to a bedroom. When I look closer, I notice a massive collection of taxidermy animals. The glass eyes all glint from the nightlight in the kitchen.

It's super creepy, but there's no sign of Mickey. The place has the air of no one being around.

I climb out of the bushes and make my way around to the back of the cabin. The moon is blocked by the woods and the back of the cabin is intensely dark. I pick my way through the yard until I find a window on the back wall.

I peer in this one, but inside is totally dark. I pull my phone from my pocket, turn on the flashlight, and look again.

I'm terrified and hopeful I will see Mickey.

All I see is a saggy bed and a dresser. A huge eagle sits on the dresser with its wings spread wide. I can't imagine what it must be like to sleep under the eagle's glare.

But there's no Mickey.

Discouraged, I check the other window. It looks in on a small bathroom, but that's all.

I step away from the cabin, confused and disappointed. I'd been so sure I'd find her here.

Good thing I didn't call 911 after all.

The wind shifts and something putrid reaches my nose. My stomach sinks at the scent of death.

Please, not Mickey.

I sniff the air, trying to determine where the scent is coming from. Once I get a direction, I hurry across the yard to the edge of the woods. The smell is strong here, behind a bush. Praying I don't see the dead body of my friend, I push the bush aside.

Entrails of some small animal, or possibly fish, lie under the bush. Flies buzz around the refuse.

My mouth waters like I may puke and I take several steps back. I'm so filled with relief that the smell isn't something horrible, I don't hear the crunching steps until they are very close.

"Rylan, is that you back here?" Declan calls.

Busted.

I walk to the front of the cabin, my mind frantically trying to think of a good reason for me to be here.

"Oh, hey," I say lamely.

"I saw someone walking across the yard, then I saw that car of yours out front." He pauses, waiting for an explanation.

I don't have one.

"Yeah, it's me. I was just..."

He raises his eyebrows when I don't finish. "Just what?"

"I don't suppose we can forget I was here."

He studies me a long moment. "Keith isn't home. Were you coming to see him?" he offers.

"Uh, yeah. I wanted to ask him a question, about, um... plants." It's a lame excuse, one I'm sure he won't believe.

He rolls his eyes just a little, then says, "Okay, keep your secrets." He takes a few steps toward the mansion. "I just finished writing for the day. Do you want to come in for a drink? I have a nice bottle of wine."

"Sure." I follow him through the woods. "So, Keith's not home. Where did he go?" I try for polite interest. Maybe he has Mickey somewhere other than the cabin. There are several out-buildings on the property.

Declan looks over his shoulder at me. "I have no idea. Why?"

I give an exaggerated shrug. "No reason. Just curious."

"About plants," he says sarcastically.

I quickly change the subject. "So, how's the writing going?"

Declan warms to this topic. "The work is great. This project is turning out better than I anticipated."

"That's wonderful." We are passing the garden. I can't keep myself from looking to the spot where Skylar died. I force my eyes away and hurry to keep up with Declan's long strides.

"I'm guessing there's no news on Mickey," he says as we enter the back door to the kitchen. When he turns on the light, the room gleams in white and stainless steel. Every surface shines, a testament to his housekeeper's skills. I'm taken aback once again by the oversized, overly modern room.

"No news. At least nothing concrete. They did find out she has a stalker," I say.

In my haste to find the truck and bearded man, I'd forgotten about the stalker angle. Was Keith the stalker?

"That's interesting. I suppose it's always possible when you're in the public eye. Would you like tea, wine, or something stronger?" He holds up a wine glass.

I'd really like a vodka tonic, and make a note I should stop by The Lock Up on my way home for a quick one. Now's not the time. "Tea, please." I sit on a stool at the wide, marble-topped bar.

He fills the wine glass for himself, then sits the bottle on the counter.

"Have you ever had trouble with a stalker like that?" I ask. "You're a public figure, too."

He turns to the refrigerator, then returns with a jug of sweet tea in his hand. He studies my face before answering. "I had a, let's say, overzealous fan once."

"Really?"

"She even came to my house. It was kind of scary."

"What happened?"

"I turned her away. Never heard from her again. Guess she didn't like me so much after that." He hands me the glass of tea and lifts his wine glass in toast. "Here's to crazy fans."

I toast with him awkwardly then take a long drink of the overly sweet liquid. I remember he always put more sugar in the tea than I liked.

"I just wish Mickey had told me about the trouble she was having. Then I could help find him."

"I'm sure she just wanted to protect you."

"I guess so. Still, if she was being harassed because of the show, I should know about it."

I run a finger along the damp side of the glass, drawing a circle. A tingle starts at the base of my spine and climbs up to my ribs. It's so strong, I flinch.

Declan sees me. "What was that? You okay?" he asks with a small laugh.

I rub my back. "I think so." I look around the room, wondering if the ghost I saw here before has returned.

The Black woman in the old-style dress stands next to the huge stainless-steel refrigerator, crouching as if she is hiding from Declan. She's motioning for my attention. I try to look without staring.

He follows my line of sight. When he turns his head, the woman ducks around the corner.

Declan looks back to me. "So what's next on the Mickey front? More sneaking around Keith's cabin?" I don't like the teasing in his tone, or the way the ghost woman is waving her hands and shaking her head in warning.

I flick my eyes to her, then back to him. He sees and his expression grows curious, excited. "Are you seeing something?"

The woman shakes her head violently, her eyes wide. "No," I lie and take another drink of tea, hoping to look casual. Something is really wrong here.

"Mr. Rathborne, you didn't tell me we had company," Anita suddenly says from the door of the kitchen. "I would have poured your drinks for you."

Declan's shoulders droop slightly as if he's annoyed. "I can manage a few drinks." There's an undercurrent in the kitchen that I don't understand.

"She has her," the ghost hisses.

Declan turns again, as if he heard the ghost speak.

I try to pretend I didn't hear. Try to pretend my heart isn't racing so hard my ears are ringing.

Did the ghost say *she?*

"Rylan, what brings you out here so late?" Anita asks, picking up a hand towel and wiping the condensation from my glass on the marble.

I have no idea how to respond. The ghost by the fridge is waving and pointing frantically and it takes all my will to not look at her.

"Anita took your friend," the ghost shouts.

Declan again looks toward the fridge as if he can hear her.

Even Anita looks, her fake smile faltering and her eyes growing dark.

"Do you know where Mickey is?" I ask, using all my courage to hold her flat, shark-like eyes.

"How would I?" she feigns innocence.

"You have to go. She's dangerous," the ghost yells.

"Just tell me where Mickey is." I stand, ready to run to save Mickey.

"So the brilliant detective's consultant figured it out," she hisses. "I heard you were too nosy for your own good."

THIRTY-EIGHT

RYLAN FLYNN

"What are you two talking about?" Declan asks. "Anita?"

I look around the room as if Mickey will appear. The ghost is yelling, "She has her in the secret room. She will hurt you. You need to run."

"Where is she?" I jump from the stool. I can't stay calm with the ghost shouting like that. "Where's the secret room?"

Her eyes widen a fraction. "That nasty ghost is here, isn't she? She's always moaning and crying and trying to get me to leave. You should have gotten rid of her the other night, like he asked, and you wouldn't be in this mess now."

"This is nuts," Declan says, slowly moving away from Anita. "Mickey isn't here."

"Oh, darling Declan, for someone so brilliant, you always were a bit obtuse."

"Rylan, you need to go. I've never seen her like this," Declan says, moving between us.

"Always with Rylan. All you can think of is her even after all this time." Anita puts her hand in her pocket. "Yeah, I know you're in love with her. I read all the things you wrote about her in that secret book you're working on. The romance novel based on your lives." She steps around the counter.

"I don't know what you're talking about," Declan tries to protest, looking from Anita to me, his face turning red.

"Last chance. Her or me?" Anita asks him.

"You? I don't understand."

"I'm the one that takes care of you every day. She's the one that broke your heart." She takes her hand from her pocket and there's a tiny pink gun in it. Tiny, but deadly just the same. "Now choose."

"Anita, seriously. This has gone too far."

She steps closer, the gun pointed at him, then at me. "Okay, obviously you won't choose me. So choose which one I shoot. You or your love?"

We both hold our hands up, slowly backing toward the door to the hall. "Anita, I choose you. I choose you."

The gun wavers a little, dips to the floor. "You do?"

"Of course. You're here for me all the time. How could I not choose you?" He turns on the charm, his accent growing thick.

"You really mean it?" He's obviously lying but she wants to believe so badly.

"I do." He takes a step forward, his hands reaching for her. At the last second, he grabs for the gun and shouts, "Run, Rylan!"

The gun raises again. "Always with Rylan!" she screams and the gun goes off.

Declan falls to the floor as Anita raises the gun at me.

The ghost is screaming full-out now. "Run!"

I take her advice, turn and sprint out of the kitchen. I encounter Evie and she begins barking wildly as I run past her. She scrambles behind me, her nails clicking on the wood floor of the hall.

"There's nowhere to run," Anita calls, too calm, following.

I slam into the front door and grab the knob. It won't turn. The door won't open.

"That's the thing about these old locks," Anita says, walking down the hall. "In or out, you need the key."

I let go of the knob and sprint up the massive stairway. I run blindly through the dark halls, as fast as I can. Each time I look over my shoulder she is near, but jogging along at a casual pace. She could shoot me at any time, I don't understand why she doesn't.

"There is nowhere in this house for you to hide," she says, not out of breath. "I know every room, every turn."

My lungs are burning and I'm already gasping for air as I make it to the second-floor stairs. I pound up them, wondering where Mickey could be and how I'm going to save her if I can't even save myself.

"Keep going," the ghost says from the top of the stairs, cheering me on.

I fly past her, Anita closing in, Evie running along with her, barking.

"What's the plan here, Rylan? You're out of floors now," she taunts.

She's right and the panic threatens to consume me. The third-floor hall is flanked with doors on either side. Most of them are open. All of them are dead ends. At the end of the hall, a door is closed. With nowhere else to go, I sprint toward it.

She's only a few steps behind me when I reach for the door. As I touch the knob, I realize this is the way to the second turret, the one that was jammed shut.

With a quick prayer, I turn the knob and the door flies open, almost knocking me over.

I pull the door shut behind me and search for a lock. There is none.

With nowhere else to go, I run up the steps to the all-glass room.

Anita opens the door and follows laughing. "Told you, you have nowhere to run. You really want me to shoot you up here? I'd rather do it while your friend watches. It's for you that I took her."

As her head comes into view above the floor, I kick at her. She grabs me by the ankle and pulls me to the floor.

"That was dumb," she says, gripping my ankle so tight the bones press into each other. "What are you going to do now that I have you?" She climbs into the room, stands over me with my ankle in her hand. "We're all alone up here."

She's wrong, the ghost is here too.

"Cover your ears," she shouts and then opens her mouth wide.

The loudest sound I've ever heard fills the room. I shove my hands hard against my ears, but it still hurts.

Even Anita seems affected and turns her head away from where the ghost is standing.

The sound goes on until the windows begin shaking. Just when the pain grows unbearable, the windows shatter, imploding. Glass slivers rain down on my face, glittering in the moonlight. Anita drops my leg in surprise, stumbles toward the top of the stairs.

The ghost continues screaming and rushes at her with hands out. At the same time, I kick with both legs.

The combined force knocks her down the steep stairs. She lands at the base of them with a heavy thud. Evie stops barking and begins to whine.

I look down at Anita crumpled at the bottom of the steps. She's breathing, but not moving, with Evie nosing at her face.

The ghost looks too. "I've wanted to do that for a long time," she tells me. "That woman is evil. Pure and simple."

"Where's Mickey?" I ask, scrambling to my feet.

"She's in the secret room in the basement. The one we used

to smuggle whiskey back in the day. Among other things during the war, long ago," she adds.

I brush broken glass off my arms and legs as I descend the stairs. I step over Anita's still body. I give her a soft kick to see if she'll wake up. She doesn't even moan. I look for the gun, but don't see it anywhere.

"Show me where Mickey is," I tell the ghost and follow her through the house.

She talks non-stop the whole way. "She's done some horrible things in this house," she says. "I'm Martha, by the way. I used to work here a long time ago. I've kept an eye on things ever since."

We reach the stairs to the second floor. "What kinds of things has she done? Did she kill Skylar?"

"She did. But she cut her first. She'd hurt her, then she'd patch her up and let her recover. Then she'd do it again. She's sick. The sickest I've ever seen."

"Why? Why hurt her over and over like that?"

"Skylar came here to see Mr. Rathborne like he said. Just showed up at his door six months ago. The poor girl was so smitten with him and was anxious to see him again. Said they met at a book signing. Anita was not pleased, but she invited the girl in. Poor thing. Didn't know what was coming."

"Mickey? What did she do to her?" I hate to ask, but I need to know.

"She's alive," is all she says before leading me to the door of the basement.

"Mickey!" I shout as I hurry down the basement stairs into the dark. "I'm here, Mickey."

I flip on the light switch and a dim light turns on. I'd imagined a large, expansive room down here. Instead, it is a warren of halls and rooms. Bare bulbs give some light in the shadows. If Martha hadn't been leading me, I would certainly have gotten lost.

"What did she want with Mickey?" I ask as we turn through the maze of walls and dirt floor.

"She told Mickey it was because she liked his books too." Martha grows silent and I stop to look at her.

"That isn't much of a reason."

"She wanted to hurt you," she says, eyes down. "To pay you back for breaking his heart."

I feel as if she's plunged a knife into my belly. "So this *is* my fault." I turn around and hurry down the hall. "Where is she?"

We take another turn and reach a blank wall. "She's here," Martha says. "Behind the secret door."

"I don't see a door."

"That's the point. You have to press at the top right and it will open."

I reach for where she said. The wood of the door is rough and old, but the corner is smooth from years of clandestine touches. I press the spot.

THIRTY-NINE

FORD PIERCE

Tyler and I leave the Speckler house after Emery and Jorgenson put the man in their car.

"If she isn't here, do you still think Rathborne is involved? Mickey having his books in her office is a thin lead at best. Lots of people have his books. Plus, she knew the guy," Tyler says as we drive away from Speckler Farm.

"We've followed weaker leads. Plus, Skylar was on his property."

"But we searched. There was nothing. And what about the beard Rylan talked about? Declan certainly doesn't have a beard."

"If the hair was fake, maybe the beard was too. Mickey would recognize him, he needed some sort of disguise."

Tyler turns this over in his mind as he drives. "I guess it won't hurt to talk to him." As we drive, I think of Rylan and what she might make of our latest idea on finding Mickey.

I go so far as to take my phone out to text her a quick check in.

I have a voice mail from her.

Instantly worried, I play the message, the phone pressed to my ear.

"Rylan thinks it's the gardener, Keith Gillespie," I tell Tyler. "She went there to see."

"She's going to get herself hurt one of these days," Tyler says, but pushes harder on the gas.

I flip on the lights and sirens. "Especially if we're right and Declan took Mickey and killed Skylar."

FORTY

RYLAN FLYNN

To my relieved surprise, the door opens a crack. I push hard against it. "Mickey?" I tuck my head into the room. It's completely dark, but I hear a rustling, then a smothered shout that sounds like my name.

I search for a light switch and flip it on. The bulb hanging from the ceiling reveals a small but horrific room. Blood stains the floor in several places. There's a cot in one corner and a bucket.

The most disturbing sight is Mickey, zip tied to a chair, blindfolded and gagged. She's slumped in the chair, but she's moving.

And screaming my name against the gag.

I hurry to her, pulling the gag out and the blindfold off at the same time.

She blinks rapidly, her eyes shocked by the light. "I knew you'd find me," she says, her voice hoarse and raspy.

"Find me something to cut her free," I tell Martha.

Mickey looks past me. "Is there someone with you?"

"A ghost named Martha. She's been helping me."

"There are knives in here. Other things too," Martha says,

pointing to a cabinet with a padlock on it. "It's locked but I know the code she uses. I've watched her open it." She gives me the numbers and I shakily spin the dial.

"Where are we?" Mickey asks. "Who?"

"We're at Declan's." I turn to her. "You don't know?"

"I've been blindfolded the whole time and he used some kind of voice modulator. I had no idea." She begins shaking. "Where is he?"

"He's unconscious, but he's not the one that's held you. His housekeeper took you." I put in the last number on the dial and pull the lock. It opens. I fling the door to the cabinet open and am met by more horror. So many tools of pain are inside. I'm momentarily stunned, but gather my wits and grab a knife.

A fake beard hangs from a nail.

At the front of the cabinet, a figurine of a farmer in a straw hat smiles at me. A wave of nausea flows through me from the figure. Evil seems to emanate from it. I smack at the figurine and it breaks against the concrete floor.

A small cloud of black smoke rises from the pile of broken ceramic.

I think of the thing locked in Keaton's room as the smoke takes shape and floats my way.

"Rylan, hurry," Mickey begs. I turn at the sound of her voice, and when I look back the smoke is gone.

I approach Mickey. "Don't move." I cut through the ties on her wrists and she rubs the red welts. I then crouch to cut her ankles from the chair. That's when I see the car battery underneath. "What did she do to you?" I whisper.

"Shocked me," Mickey says. "Just get me out of here."

I shake my head in disgust and cut her free.

She instantly springs to her feet, but then sits back down. "My legs are weak." She stretches them out in front of her.

"Lean on me. Let's get you out of here."

Mickey stands shakily and I help her out of the room.

We wind through the halls, Martha again leading the way.

The dim lights suddenly go out.

"She's awake," Martha says.

"Rylan, you shouldn't have come here," Anita's voice calls through the dark. Mickey grabs my arm, squeezes tight.

"Don't let her find us," she whispers into my ear as we cower against a wall in the consuming dark.

"I won't," I assure her, though I have no idea which way to go in the complete darkness, let alone how to save us. I think briefly of Ford and hope he got my message. Of course that will only lead him to the gardener's cabin, not to this dank and dark basement.

"Come this way," Martha says. "Just follow my voice."

I step toward the sound. Mickey holds my hand and follows. Our steps sound too loud on the dirt floor. My breathing seems to scream through the dark, giving our location away. We shuffle along like this for what seems a long time.

Anita calls every few moments. Sometimes she sounds closer, sometimes farther away.

"You know, this is all your fault," Anita says. "If it wasn't for you, I'd never have started this marvelous journey."

"Just focus on me," Martha coaxes. "Don't listen to a word she says. I'll get you out." I trust the ghost and I lead Mickey until we enter a space that seems larger than the others. There is a small square of light on one of the walls.

"It's the dumbwaiter," Martha says. "It will take you up to the kitchen."

I tell Mickey the plan and we walk toward the light. "I'll send you up first."

"I can't leave you here," she protests, gripping my arm so tight it hurts.

"Soon as you climb out, just send it back down and I'll follow."

"We need to go together." Her panic rises.

"There isn't room for us both. Just go." I find the handle and open the box. It's like a tiny elevator that goes to the kitchen and other levels of the house. A faint light from above fills the box.

Mickey climbs in. I shove my phone into her hand. "Once you get out, call 911."

"I'm so sorry, Rylan. I love you," she says as she climbs into the dumbwaiter.

"I love you too, but go." I pull the hatch closed on her then press the button that should take her to the kitchen.

The dumbwaiter squeals on its way up.

There's a moment of silence, then a thunder of footsteps. "I got you," Anita says as she steps into the room. The light of her phone shines in my face.

"You don't want to do this," I tell her, trying to buy time. "You won't get away with it."

"As long as I get you, I don't care."

"Why do you hate me so much? We don't even know each other."

"You have Declan's heart, that's all I need to know."

"You're sick. None of this is my fault."

"Isn't it? Mickey is here because of you."

I'm backed against the wall now, and the dumbwaiter. Why hasn't Mickey sent it back down?

"She has the gun," Martha says, her voice full of fear.

Behind me, the dumbwaiter finally squeals again, returning to the basement. It's too late. Anita would surely shoot me if I try to climb inside.

"Tell you what," she says. "You come to my play room and I'll let Mickey go. I'd rather have you anyway. You're the reason he doesn't love me after all."

"If you love him, why did you shoot him?"

"Don't worry, I didn't aim to kill. Daddy taught me where to aim."

"I'll never go with you."

The light grows ever closer to my face. "Do you really think you have a choice?"

Just then, the door of the dumbwaiter flies open and a shadow springs past me, screaming. It's Mickey.

The light in my face drops to the floor, glints off the butcher knife in Mickey's hand.

The gun goes off, the light from the muzzle temporarily blinding me.

"Mickey!" I yell.

Anita calls out in pain.

Mickey screams like a wild woman. The glinting knife raises, then something hot and wet hits me in the face.

Anita falls quiet and Mickey stops screaming.

The silence is deafening.

Somehow, the basement lights switch back on in that moment, illuminating a horror scene. Mickey straddles Anita's still body. She turns her face to me and it's covered in blood. She's staring at the knife, as though surprised to see it. It tumbles from her wet fingers to the dirt floor.

"She shot me," she says, her face pleading for help, then collapses next to the knife.

I hurry to her side, check for a pulse in her neck. Her heart beats, but not evenly.

I press my hands to the hole in her shoulder. "Stay with me. Stay with me."

A sick sense of déjà vu fills my mind as her blood seeps through my fingers.

"Rylan?" Distantly, I hear Ford calling my name.

"Here!" I shout. "We're here. We need an ambulance."

I hear the crackle of his radio as he calls for help, the sound growing stronger as he gets nearer.

I sit with Mickey, putting pressure on her wound.

"Anita's moving," Martha says, standing close.

Anita stirs, her hand reaching toward the gun lying in the dirt.

Stretching my leg out, I kick the gun away from her hand and she collapses again.

I turn my focus to Mickey and her breathing. "Please don't go," I beg. "I need you. I've always needed you." I cannot imagine watching Mickey leave her body, watching the light open up to take her. "Stay with me," I sob.

Mickey moans slightly, the greatest sound I've ever heard.

Ford suddenly rushes into the room with Tyler close behind. Their eyes fly wide at the scene. They look from Anita's bloody body to Mickey's.

"Anita shot Mickey," I say miserably. "She needs help."

Ford checks Anita for a pulse. "Still beating," he says.

Tyler drops to the floor and presses his hands to the hole in Mickey's shoulder, moving mine away. Ford helps me stand. "Are you hurt?" he wipes at Anita's blood on my face.

"No." I look at Anita lying unconscious and bleeding. I'm curiously void of emotion. "It was all her. She killed Skylar and took Mickey."

Ford presses my face to his chest. "You're safe now."

I sink into his arms and start shaking from shock. "I'm so glad you came," I say. He squeezes me tighter. I allow myself a moment of comfort then pull away and drop back to Mickey's side.

Ford tends to Anita's injuries. I can't look.

We wait in the dirty basement for help to arrive.

I suddenly remember Declan. "She shot Declan," I shout. Making sure Mickey is well taken care of by Tyler, I run from the room.

"Show me the way out," I tell Martha.

"Rylan, wait!" Ford follows.

We finally reach the basement stairs and I pound up them. "Declan," I shout, saying a silent prayer he is okay.

He lies on his back in the kitchen, a pool of blood around him on the stark white tile. I drop to my knees by his side. His eyes flutter open and meet mine.

"She shot me," he says, his accent heavy and slurred.

"We saved Mickey," I tell him. He's bleeding from a shot to his thigh. There's a lot of blood oozing out.

"I didn't know she was here. I swear."

"I know you didn't. You'd never do that."

Ford gives me the hand towel Anita used earlier. "Here, put pressure on it."

Declan isn't bleeding as badly as Skylar or Mickey, but his blood still soaks my hands.

"I'm so sorry, Declan. Anita did this all because of me."

"You can't blame yourself," Ford says sternly behind my shoulder.

I turn to him. "Can't I? She said she took Mickey to hurt me because she was jealous."

"Anita made her own decisions."

"If that's what you think." I press harder on the wound in Declan's thigh and he moans.

"Not so hard," he exclaims.

"Sorry," I say.

"I'm glad you're here," Declan says tenderly, reaching to brush a strand of hair from my face.

The gentle gesture feels awkward with Ford watching, but when I look back Ford has left the room.

In the distance, sirens sing.

FORTY-ONE

RYLAN FLYNN

"They won't let me in to see her," I tell Mom when she asks how Mickey is doing the next day.

"That's silly. You're her best friend. She needs you." Mom knows the basic outline of what happened, but I don't think she grasps all the implications.

Mickey's parents, as well as Marco, have made it clear I am not welcome at the hospital to visit. They completely blame me.

That's okay, I blame myself. Maybe Mickey is safer without me.

But wondering about her is really getting to me. I know she's safe, but is she okay? I mean really okay? Who knows what Anita did to her while she held her captive.

I'm one of the few people Mickey knows that can relate. We could help each other.

No amount of comforting talk from Mom's ghost or wise words from Dad makes the guilt go away. The only one that might make me feel better is Mickey, but I can't get to her.

Late on day two, I can't take it anymore and head to the hospital, hoping to catch her in her room alone.

I open the hospital room door and duck my head in. She's lying in the bed, her face pale. "Can I come in?" I ask nervously.

"Of course. I figured you'd come before. Where have you been?" she asks, trying for a teasing tone, but failing.

"I—I wanted to. They—"

She reaches a hand for mine. "You're here now. That's all that matters."

"So you're not mad at me?" I ask in disbelief.

"Why would I be mad? I know my parents are blaming you. Trust me, they've told me lots of times. And I keep telling them that what happened wasn't your fault."

I sink into the chair next to her bed. She looks tired and in pain. "Does it hurt much?" I ask.

She gives me wry smile. "What do you think? It's not pleasant." She touches her bandaged shoulder. I see bandages on her arms, too. She sees me staring.

"Electrical burns," she says, then hides her arms under the blanket. "Just like in one of Declan's books."

Tears prick my eyes. "I'm so sorry," I say. "I can't even—"

"Have you seen her?" Mickey finally asks.

"She's being held under guard down the hall. She'll survive."

Mickey sits back, closes her eyes. "I don't know how to feel about that."

"I can't imagine. I just don't understand how she did this to you."

She opens her eyes and they meet mine. There's a quiet strength in her expression. "I'm still here," she says. "I still have you and Marco and my family. That's what truly matters."

As if summoned, Marco enters the room. He looks from me to Mickey, anger in his eyes. "I thought we told you not to visit."

"Rylan is my best friend," Mickey says. "She saved me."

"She put you in danger."

"Enough! Anita Monroe put me in danger. No one is to blame except her," she says firmly.

"I should go," I say, standing and making my way to the door.

"You'll come back? They say I can go home tomorrow. Maybe we should discuss the future of the show."

"You want to come back?"

"You try and stop me. After all this, what's the worst that can happen?" She smiles and my heart lifts for the first time in days.

A few days later, I'm sitting on Mom's bed watching old reruns of *ALF*. The fuzzy alien still makes Mom laugh. Anything that can bring her joy is good to me. I've visited Mickey twice since she went home from the hospital. Both times, Marco watched us closely, still not ready to forgive me for what happened.

I can only hope time will soften him. We haven't discussed continuing the show yet and I've talked to Aunt Val about working at The Hole in case the show ends. I've helped out a few times in the past, but this is different. Still, I'm thankful for the opportunity.

When Val calls, I assume it's about the job.

"I was wondering if I could ask you a favor," she says, surprising me.

"Of course," I say, stepping out into the hall so Mom can watch her show in peace.

"I really hate to ask after all you've been through."

"I could use the diversion. I'm literally watching reruns right now." I don't tell her I'm with Mom.

"Um, do you think we could finish our encounter with Justin? I know it's a lot to ask."

Guilt swamps me. I haven't thought about Justin or Aunt

Val's quest to talk to him. I should have. "Of course. I'd love to. Is tonight okay?"

"I'll call Sawyer and have him come."

I hear something tender in the way she says his name. "How are things with you two?"

She takes a moment to answer. "Declan has been staying with him while he recovers, but we've also been spending a lot of time together. Is it bad to say that we're happy? It's like we were never apart, but this time it's different. Do you know what I mean?"

I actually don't, but I can imagine so I say, "Sure. I'm glad you found each other at last."

"I just want Justin to be happy too. If we can help him cross over, maybe he can find peace."

"I'll be over tonight."

The night is perfect for contacting a spirit. The moon is full and bright, with only a few clouds in the sky. There's the slightest breeze in the clearing when I arrive at Aunt Val's.

She and Sawyer are already on the porch, sitting side by side in the rockers.

They look comfortable together and that makes me happy.

And a little sad, if I'm truthful.

I haven't seen Ford since the night at the mansion. Without a case to work on, there doesn't seem to be a reason for us to talk. Did I imagine how close we have become? Is it only fueled by the adrenaline of the chase? These are questions I don't want to investigate.

Val stands when I walk up the steps to the porch. "You ready for this?" she asks.

"Hello to you, too," I say with a smile.

"Sorry, I'm just nervous." She looks to Sawyer for support.

Sawyer smiles at me and places a hand on Val's shoulder. "Now don't be so scared. This will be good."

"Of course," she says, putting her hand on his. "I'm just—"

"I know. It's okay. So am I."

"How's Declan?" I ask him. "I should have visited, but you know..."

Sawyer runs a hand over his face and looks into the woods. "His leg is healing, but his heart is sick. He feels so responsible for what happened to Skylar and Mickey. If Anita hadn't been obsessed with him..." He looks back at Val and his face softens.

Looks like Declan and I have guilt in common.

"Any word on Keith? Ford said he was pretty upset Anita tried to frame him."

"He was pretty upset but he's decided to stay at Krieger."

"That's good." I change the subject. "Well, let's get to it. Want to do it in the woods again or in the clearing?"

"He came to the woods the first time," Val says, giving Sawyer a gentle look.

I lead them a short distance into the trees then stop. "This looks like a good place," I say. We join hands in a small circle and I look to the sky. Through the gaps of the branches I can see the moon.

"Lord, please let us do what Justin needs. Justin, if you are out there, please come talk to us," I say.

This time it doesn't take long for him to appear. "I'm here." He sounds much stronger than last time, although he's not much more than a mist in the dark. "Valerie, you brought Sawyer."

"He's here," I tell them and repeat what he said.

"I did like you said," Val says. "We're here together."

"That's all I wanted for you, to not be alone."

I tell them what he said.

Val looks to Sawyer and they exchange a smile. "We're not alone any longer," Val says. "Thank you for looking after me all this time. I never saw you, but I felt your presence. It means the world to me."

"You mean the world to me," Justin says and I repeat it.

Val chokes up. "I loved you, Justin. And I'm so sorry for what happened. If I hadn't been messing around..."

"Stop that. It was an accident, plain and simple."

"But, if only—" Val stops.

"If onlys get you nowhere," Justin says. "Just hold onto each other. That will make me happy."

I tell them what he said.

"You are such a good man. You always were." Val's voice breaks. "But you need to go on. You need to cross over."

"I can help you," I tell Justin's misty shape.

"Now that I know you are okay, that you are not alone, I can go."

When I tell them he's ready, Val sniffles.

I start saying the prayer Dad normally says. Soon the familiar block of light opens behind him, so bright it hurts my eyes.

"You'll take care of her for me?" Justin asks Sawyer.

I relay the question and Sawyer answers, "We'll take care of each other."

"That's all I've waited for," Justin says soberly. His form takes a step back and the light absorbs him.

"Goodbye, Justin," Val whispers, her voice breaking.

"He's crossed," I say and let go of their hands. I feel oddly empty. It happened so quickly, it's kind of scary to think a soul can leave so fast after being on this side for so long. I can't help thinking about Mom.

"Is he really gone?" Sawyer asks. "How do you know?"

"I saw the light take him."

"There's really a light? How fascinating." Sawyer studies me. "This whole ghost thing is so interesting."

"It's something. I didn't ask for the gift, but I'm glad when I can help the spirits. And when they can help me." I think of Martha and all the help she gave me. I went back to the mansion last night, wanting to see her again. I stood outside on the portico and called to her, but she didn't show. I'd like to help her cross, too, but I get the feeling she's content to look after the house.

Val squeezes my upper arm in affection. "Thank you, Rylan. Truly, thank you."

"Glad to do it," I say honestly, and start walking toward my car.

"Do you want to stay a while? I could make snacks."

"I'm sorry, I should be going." I notice Sawyer has taken Val's hand. "I'm sure you two have a lot to catch up on."

Val smiles. "We do."

I lean in and give her a quick hug. "Good night."

She pulls me in tight. "Be careful."

"I always am," I say with forced brightness.

I check my phone twice on my way home, hopelessly wondering if Ford will call. It's late, but his life doesn't run on a regular schedule. I tell myself that he's been busy wrapping up the case against Anita.

After I park in the driveway, I decide to get the mail before going into my packed full, but empty, house.

Among the regular junk mail is a letter with a strange return address.

The county jail.

Curious, I tear the letter open.

Dear Rylan Flynn,

You probably don't remember me. My name is Andrea and we went to summer camp together at Lakewood. I've seen your show and I heard you also help the police sometimes. I need your help, and can't go to the authorities.

I'm in jail for a murder I didn't commit. I'm being framed, and I think you may be the only one who can save me. Please come visit me so I can explain.

Andrea Evans

I search my vague memories of camp for an Andrea Evans. It was a long time ago, but a memory of a skinny blond in a canoe comes to mind. Before I can completely digest the contents of the letter, my phone rings.

Absently, I pull my phone from my pocket.

It's Ford.

A LETTER FROM DAWN

Dearest reader,

A huge thank you for choosing to read *The Whisper House*. I truly appreciate you picking my story to spend time with. I hope you loved it. If you did enjoy it, and want to keep up to date with all my latest releases, just sign up at the following link. Your email address will never be shared and you can unsubscribe at any time.

www.secondskybooks.com/dawn-merriman

Writing *The Whisper House* was quite a ride. It went through a few different versions and major edits before the story came together. As usual, Rylan kept me on my toes and threw me for some loops. I hope you love how it all turned out.

If you enjoyed *The Whisper House*, I would be very grateful if you could leave a review. Feedback from readers is so special. I'd love to hear what you think, and it makes such a difference helping new readers to discover one of my books for the first time.

I love hearing from my readers and I interact on my Fan Club on Facebook at the link below. Join the club today and get behind-the-scenes info on my works, fun games and interesting tidbits from my life.

www.facebook.com/groups/dawnmerrimannovelistfanclub

Again, thank you for reading *The Whisper House.*

Happy reading and God bless,

Dawn Merriman

 facebook.com/dawnmerrimannovelist
instagram.com/dawnmerrimannovelist

ACKNOWLEDGMENTS

This book would not be possible without the help from "my team."

First, I'd like to thank my husband, Kevin whose help and insights are invaluable.

To my beta reader team, Carlie Frech, Katie Hoffman, Jamie Miller, Candy Wajer and Marjie Spencer. I love nothing more than discussing the books with you guys.

A huge thank you to Bookouture, Second Sky Books, and the wonderful team there. Your faith in me and in Rylan is wonderful. To my editor, Jack Renninson, I truly appreciate all you've done for *The Whisper House*. It is a better book because of your input.

Thank you to my readers for choosing my stories to spend time with.

Most of all, thank you to God for giving me the gift to tell the stories. I hope I do them justice.

Thank you all,

Dawn Merriman

PUBLISHING TEAM

Turning a manuscript into a book requires the efforts of many people. The publishing team at Bookouture would like to acknowledge everyone who contributed to this publication.

Audio
Alba Proko
Sinead O'Connor
Melissa Tran

Commercial
Lauren Morrissette
Jil Thielen
Imogen Allport

Cover design
Damonza.com

Data and analysis
Mark Alder
Mohamed Bussuri

Editorial
Jack Renninson
Melissa Tran

Printed in Great Britain
by Amazon

52324634R10131